Other books by Ian Cordery, which are all available from Amazon, in Kindle, and Paperback formats.

Out there, Somewhere

Lifeblood

Spectral Fear

The Zone of Light (Extended Version)

Inferus, the Dark Lands (The Zone of Light 2)

Coming soon:

Shadow People

For more details, and news of future books, please check the link below:

https://www.facebook.com/groups/8764747 03279526/

ECHOES: (AN ANTHOLOGY OF SHORT STORIES)

By Ian Cordery

Copyright © 2022

ECHOES: (AN ANTHOLOGY OF SHORT STORIES)

IAN CORDERY

Chapters: (1 - 8)

Chapters: (9 - 16)

1: COUNTDOWN

In April 2021, Ray Ashdown, aged 70 and retired, was diagnosed with Bowel Cancer, and his life was about to change.

After various tests, he was admitted to the Royal Surrey Hospital, in Guildford in May, just 3-weeks after the diagnosis.

Ray lost his wife Julie to Pancreatic Cancer in 2015, and he had discussed the details of the surgery with his three children, but pointed out that he would need the operation in order to survive, but also, that there could be complications.

After waiting for a couple of hours, following a "pre-op", and blood tests, he was admitted to the theatre, where a team of surgeons and nurses were waiting for him, to run through the procedures, before commencing.

A canula had already been fitted into a vein on his right arm, and secured with a plaster, during the "pre-op" procedure. A nurse injected some liquid into the canula; Ray could feel the liquid getting warm, and was told by the nurse that it would make him start to feel drowsy; then she asked Ray to countdown from 20!

'20, 19, 18 …' Ray then drifted into a deep sleep.

Ray awoke, and looked around the room, which he assumed was a ward, but he was fully dressed, and was seated next to two other people; he was seated in an aircraft that was about to take off, and wondered what was happening. He didn't want to upset anyone, due to being on a plane, and started to panic, but thought to himself, as the aircraft taxied along the runway. *'I cannot alert anyone, the flight crew are already seated for take-off, so I must think about what to do next, without making a scene, and causing others to panic!'*

The plane took off from the North Terminal, at London Gatwick Airport; Ray noticed that the lady sitting next to him, was reading a book, which was about Cyprus, and wondered whether this was to be his destination. He checked his pockets, and found his passport in his jacket pocket; he also saw that he had his mobile phone with him, which was switched to "Flight-Mode", so somehow, he must have known that he was going to fly somewhere, but couldn't remember how?

Ray was widowed six years ago, after being married to his childhood sweetheart Julie, for 44 years; together, they had three children, and four grandchildren, Ray was so proud of everyone. He retired from his employment at the end of March 2021, after working as an Electrical Engineer for a large company, over a forty-year period. Ray was a popular employee and had managed to help grow the company, during the years he was there.

He drifted off, and what felt like a few minutes later, was suddenly tapped on his shoulder by an attractive Air Stewardess, confirming that he should buckle his seatbelt, as they were shortly due to land. Ray was still wondering what he was doing on this flight, alone?

(This flight from memory, he recalled, takes over four hours, and thought to himself, what is happening?') As he buckled his seatbelt, he thought about one of the many holidays he'd had with his late wife, then the plane screeched onto the long runway; Ray glanced across at the terminal and knew then, that he was in Paphos, a place he knew well!

He disembarked and followed the other passengers across to the Terminal, where he went through passport control very quickly, then into the baggage area. (*'Baggage, do I have any bags,' he mumbled?'*)

Ray checked the carousel, and noticed that there was a large black suitcase with a green belt tied around it. (*'This was Julie's case he thought, this is the one I bought her for Xmas, a few months before she passed away, what the hell is going on here?'*) Then he could feel a single tear falling from his left eye. Ray picked up his case, and went through to security, then into the arrivals, when he suddenly felt alone, and panic started to set in. *'Where am I going, why am I here, and alone, he mumbled?'*

Ray aimlessly walked through the arrival's hall, then repeated, *'Where am I going, why am I here and why am I on my own?'*) He then spotted a man holding up a card with his name printed on it; he nodded at the man who then called out, 'Are you Mr Ashdown?' Ray looked at the Cypriot man, who confirmed his name. *'Hello, I am Costas, welcome to Paphos, I have your taxi parked close by!'* He got into the Taxi, and was about to ask questions, but Costas informed him that he was taking him to the "Cypria Maris" Hotel, close to the seafront, which was only about 25-minutes away.

(*'The hotel where Julie and I spent our last holiday together', now I am really baffled'*) Ray didn't want to ask the driver any questions, so he remained quiet, for the rest of the journey.

Costas dropped him off at the entrance to the magnificent "5-Star" hotel, and confirmed that the fare had been paid for by Carol; Ray was about to question the driver, but felt he was in a hurry to get his next fare, but chuckled, when he was given a smile, which revealed a lot of gold teeth.

After checking in, he was taken to a very large suite, which was big enough for at least four people; the porter placed Ray's case onto a rack; Ray checked his pockets and found some Euro's, then gave the porter a ten-euro note, which was gratefully received by the young-looking hotel employee, who passed the keys over to him, and asked him to contact room service, if he needed anything.

He opened the case, hoping he could remember packing it and also, to see what he had actually packed. There was a knock on the door, which made Ray jump; he opened the heavy wooden door, and saw a beautiful lady standing outside. 'Hi Ray, so glad you could make it, it is really good to see you again.' Ray was dumbfounded, '*who was this very attractive lady and how does she know me*?'

'You had better come in, said Ray, we need to talk, I need to know what is happening here!' They sat at a table by the window, which overlooked a large swimming pool below; Ray slightly stuttered. '*Y-you must forgive me madam; I have had a long flight and ...'*

'Ray, don't worry, I know how hard it's been for you,

since you lost Julie, so let me confirm the situation.'
'Who was this very attractive lady, Ray wondered, and how does she know me?'

'My name is Carol, we met two years ago, just after your operation for Cancer, which was at the same hospital, where my husband had passed away, and you were in the same ward. We spoke briefly and you told me about your late wife and your love of Cyprus, so we met for coffee in Woking, when you were discharged, as we both lived close by. Sadly, as you know, my husband Stephen didn't make it, and you were so comforting at a time I needed someone to talk to. I moved to Cyprus after spending some time with friends, and we eventually arranged to meet here today, after making many lengthy telephone calls.

'Wait, sorry Carol, this all sounds amazing, but I cannot remember anything, except that Cyprus was the last holiday I spent with my late wife, and also, I cannot remember much about the operation, or waking up afterwards?'

'Ray, don't worry, it will all come back to you, let's go and get a drink in the harbour, then we can talk in more detail. They left the room and picked up a waiting taxi outside the hotel. 'The Harbour please,' Carol stated to the driver.

Ray remembered the Harbour Area, the Fort and the vast number of restaurants he had frequented, with his late wife Julie, the last time he was in Cyprus

'A large Keo and a Vodka and tonic please,' said Ray to the waiter; 'So, Ray, you remember my favourite drink,' Carol remarked. *'It was also Julie's favourite, Ray replied, 'Sorry!'*

After talking for a long time, and eating some fresh seafood, Ray was still unaware of how he had managed to get to Cyprus, and hoped that Carol would be able to confirm the details. 'We met up just after my late husband Stephen passed away, said Carol, and it was a purely platonic relationship at first, but eventually, we decided that we wanted to get move things on, so we became more intimate.' (*'Surely, I would have remembered going to bed with such a beautiful lady,' Ray thought*) 'Stephen and I had purchased a house in Coral Bay, where we would have settled down, once he retired, but he became ill and was diagnosed with bowel cancer, and unfortunately, they didn't catch the cancer very quickly; then Stephen encountered a few problems, and passed away shortly after the operation.'

'I am so sorry for your loss carol, Ray remarked. (*'I am sure I must have already conveyed my condolences to Carol,' he thought.*)

'We got on so well, continued Carol, and decided to move into your house after a year together, so I rented my place out. We had a few trips to Spain and Florida, and I told you about the house in Coral Bay, so we both agreed that we would not go there, until we were fully over our grieving; and now we are here as planned.'

They went for a walk along the sea front, and Ray agreed to go and see Carol's house in Coral Bay. A taxi took them along the coastal road and Ray started to remember quite a few of the landmarks.

'I remember eating at that restaurant over there with Julie, said Ray, Julie loved the "Tavas", a Cypriot stew of braised beef, potatoes and herbs, and she would eat the stew, even when the weather was very hot!'

In Coral Bay, the taxi took them past the "Strip", which was a road full of restaurants, bars and shops, then continued down towards the sea front, then onto a private road.

The taxi pulled up, outside a magnificent looking, gated house. 'This is it,' cried Carol, this is our retirement home!' *"Retirement home"*, thought Ray, is this place full of retired pensioners?'

Carol showed him round the Six-bedroomed property, but Ray asked why there were so many bedrooms. 'Well, we have six grandchildren between us darling, and everyone will be welcome here,' announced Carol.

Ray started to wonder if everything was a dream, there were so many things happening, all good of course, and everything he ever wanted with his late wife Julie. (*'I'm going to wake up shortly, and realise this was only a dream,' Ray thought*)

They had dinner that evening, at the Andria Steak House along "the Strip" and managed to finish two bottles of red wine, so they spent the evening at Carol's house; it had been a long day, and Ray fell asleep, as soon as his head touched the pillow; Carol kissed him on his forehead and whispered 'Goodnight my darling'!

The following morning, Ray awoke and saw the sun coming through the blinds, he looked at Carol lying next to him and immediately remarked; *'such a beautiful lady'!* He made went down to the kitchen, where he made some coffee and toast, then took them into the bedroom. 'Breakfast in bed darling, how wonderful', said Carol.

Ray was starting to come round after his surgery, the nurse spoke to him and asked how he felt. Ray was

feeling quite groggy, but managed to smile at the nurse.
'You are in the recovery ward Ray, the nurse confirmed,
just relax and shortly, we will take you to the main
ward'. Ray's eyes became heavy, and he drifted off to
sleep.

He woke up, and was lying next to Carol. (*What is
going on he thought to himself, I was in the hospital just
a minute ago, and now I am back in Cyprus with
Carol?'*) 'You must be so tired darling, stated Carol,
please go back to sleep, just rest, we have all the time in
the world!'

Ray awoke and looked around the room, he was now
in the main ward at the Guildford Hospital. (*'So, it was
all a dream, he mumbled; shame, I would love to be back
in Cyprus with Carol'*)

There were five other beds in the ward, with only two
of them occupied; the nurse asked Ray how he was
feeling, and whether he would like some lunch. 'Just a
coffee please nurse,' he replied. He drank the coffee and
laid back on the pillow, then drifted in and out of sleep,
but each time, he awoke in the hospital ward.

Visiting was restricted, due to the Covid rules, but
Ray had spoken to each of his three children and four
grandchildren, confirming that he was ok.

He spotted a very glamourous lady walking into the
ward, who greeted the man in the bed to his right. 'How
are you Stephen', she said. Ray could see it was Carol,
even though she had a mask covering her lower face.
Her husband seemed to be quite poorly and Ray started
thinking. *'How can this be, how would I know about
what happens in the future, and that her husband would
pass away, then she would eventually move to Cyprus,*

where we will meet, and would become more than friends?'

Ray and Carol did get together; everything he had dreamt about came true; they got married in Cyprus several years after settling down in Coral Bay; the wedding was held in a strange Church in a small village called Pachyammos, close to the Turkish-Cypriot border, attended by Rays three children, his four grandchildren. Carols daughter and two children were also there, and everyone got on very well, with all of their children happy that their parents had again, found love, after the pain they had both gone through.

After the wedding ceremony, they had booked a restaurant for everyone, in a nearby resort called Pomos, which they had chosen, as it overlooked the harbour and had a wonderful view of the sea and the mountains. Carol made sure that all their guests were happy, and told them that they were welcome to stay at their house, whenever they wanted to come over.

After a few speeches, the small gathering toasted the bride and groom. (*Carol whispered to Ray, 'cheers darling, and let's raise our glasses to both our late partners, my Stephen, and your Julie!'*)

Ray and Carol Ashdown spent the rest of their lives, living happily together, in Coral Bay, but always spoke about their late partners.

2: THE LOVERS

The room was filled with the most wonderful music, then Maddy Prior started to sing. She sang the adapted words, to the song of Hiawatha, which haunted the listener; he was in awe of the music by Mike Oldfield, the words by Henry Wadsworth Longfellow, and the story it told, of Hiawatha and Minnehaha.

He played the 17-minute, final track, of side two, from the "Incantations" vinyl album, over and over again, until he was able to recite them, word for word.

"By the shore of Gitche Gumee,
By the shining Big-Sea-Water,
At the doorway of his wigwam,
In the pleasant summer morning,
Hiawatha stood and waited".

David Randall was 20 years old; he was out of work and lived on handouts, from the government and also, from his loving parents. He had regular interviews for possible employment, but each time, was considered not suitable for the position on offer, so he spent most of his time river fishing, close to his parent's home in Kingston, Surrey.

With the help from his parents, David purchased a computer, and some specialist decks, speakers and a microphone. He practiced on his new equipment every day, until finally, he was confident he could find the odd "gig", as a Disc-Jockey.

He placed an advert in the Surrey Comet newspaper and was amazed by the enquiries he received.

His first booking was for a wedding, which was held in the Richmond Hill Hotel, close to Richmond Park. He asked a close friend, who had a small van, to help him transport and set up the equipment and arrived an hour before the wedding guests, were due to arrive.

The night went well, the music he played, was enjoyed by all the attending guests and he even managed to get a couple of further bookings, both in close proximity to his home in Kingston.

Two weeks later, he arrived at his next booking, which was secured, following his debut gig, at Richmond Hill. His friend Kevin, helped him unload and set up the equipment, but couldn't stay, as he had a prior engagement. David had agreed to store his equipment at the venue and would return to pick it up, the following day.

The guests started to arrive, for the 21st Birthday party, at the Cobham Rugby Club, between Cobham and Esher. David was introduced to Lauretta, by her father, who confirmed that his daughter was really looking forward to this special evening and hoped he would make it a night to remember, for her, and even paid David's fee straight away, including an additional £50, to make sure the evening was a success.

As the guests were arriving, he played some background music, so that they could meet and greet each other and talk about old times. He gradually increased the sound and played his favourite track, part 4 from the Mike Oldfield album, Incantations. Several of the guests asked what the track was and who by?

The Tamla Motown music went down well, the floor was packed, so David was happy that he'd managed to please the crowd and didn't want the evening to end.

He played the Lionel Ritchie track, "Three times a Lady", for the last dance, and noticed that Lauretta wasn't dancing. He looked at her and gestured, asking if she would like to dance, and she agreed. He asked her why she wasn't dancing with her boyfriend, but she didn't answer. As they danced, all she said was "love your accent", in her Texan drawl.

David received a call from Lauretta, the following day, thanking him for such a brilliant evening;; she apologised for not responding to his question last night, and confirmed that she and her boyfriend had been arguing, for a long time, but had now finished with him.

Lauretta Arnold lived with her parents, at their 8-bedroomed house in Cobham, Surrey. Gregg Arnold, her father, was from Waco, Texas, and owned businesses in the UK, America and parts of Europe, relating to the oil industry; he was a multi-millionaire. Jennifer Arnold, Lauretta's mother, worked part-time, at the American Community School, also in Cobham, teaching dance and fitness lessons.

Lauretta worked in London, close to Oxford Circus, where she ran a successful retail clothing business, which was a gift from her father, on her eighteenth birthday.

David met Lauretta at the Black Swan pub in Cobham, not far from where she lived, a week after their phone call. They spoke about everything and everyone, places they had visited, what their goals were, their relationships and about their parents.

David told the truth, and said he had only been on one date before now, but that it didn't work out. He also confirmed that he was looking for work and would hopefully, one day, visit places, which for now, he could only dream of.

Lauretta clasped his hand and stated that maybe his dreams would come true, one day.

Their relationship blossomed, and after speaking to her parents, Lauretta invited David over for dinner.

Gregg Arnold greeted David with a firm handshake, and asked him to come and get a drink. Gregg spoke about his business ventures across the world, then asked David what he did for work. He wasn't amused when David told him that he was currently looking for work, but for the sake of not embarrassing his guest, he slapped him on his back and led him back to the dining room, where dinner was being served, by a waitress and a butler. 'Another world', thought David.

After dinner, Gregg offered David a very large cigar, and a glass of warmed cognac; David accepted the cognac, but politely stated that he didn't smoke.

Later that evening, David left the large house and

hoped that he'd been accepted by Lauretta's parents, but once he had gone, the arguments started.

'That boy is not right for you, said Gregg Arnold; he is not working and has no property, no prospects and furthermore, he is not welcome here!'

Lauretta ran upstairs to her bedroom and cried. Her mother knocked silently on her door and entered. She apologised for her father's outburst and said he would come round eventually.

'You know what he's like darling,' she said.

'Yes, I *do* mother,' replied Lauretta.

Jennifer Arnold left her daughter, who was still in floods of tears.

David met Lauretta for lunch in a pub, close to her business in Margaret Street, London, a few days later. She mentioned that her father was not happy with their relationship, but stated that she was now 21 years old and did not need his permission, and couldn't give a damn! He kissed her, then gripped her hand and said thank you.

'Have you anything planned for this evening,' asked Lauretta. Why don't we see what's on at the cinema and have dinner after?'

'Sounds good to me, said David, but let's go Dutch, if you don't mind!'

They stayed in London and watched a film at the Odeon, in Leicester Square, then went for dinner, at the Indian restaurant Dishoom, in St Martins Lane. The food was better than anything David had eaten from his local curry "take-away", and the wine was perfect. Lauretta paid the bill and said they could sort it out later.

'Would you mind staying with me this evening, asked

Lauretta. I don't want to go home, so we can stay at a hotel for the night, rather than make the boring train journey, back to Cobham. Don't worry, daddy has an account in most of the top London hotel's, he won't mind!'

They checked in at the Savoy Hotel, David was amazed at the "Art-Deco" Architecture, the lighting, and the smartly dressed staff.

'Welcome Miss Arnold, said the Hotel Manager, good to see you, and please convey my thanks to your father, for his kindness, when he was last here.'

After a nightcap in the famous American Bar, they took the lift to the top floor and entered their room. David was scared, he had never had an intimate relationship with a girl before, and sleeping in the same bed! 'Oh well,' he thought!

They made love for most of the night and into the early hours of the morning. They both confessed to each other, that it was their first time, and agreed it was very special.

Lauretta managed not to speak about her liaison with David, to her parents and hoped that nothing further would be said, but her father had recently spoken to the Savoy Hotel Manager, about some other business.

The argument with her father got heated and ended up with Lauretta, running up to her bedroom, again! Rather than let it get any worse, Lauretta decided to speak to her father, to try and make him understand.

'Don't you want me to be happy, said Lauretta, I didn't want this to happen, but I have fallen in love with David and we want to be together, for the rest of our lives!'

'You just don't understand young lady, said her father in response; he is not working; he has no intention of working, and if you let him, he will rely on *your* income, to support what *he* wants. Now, why don't you forget about him and find someone who *will* be more supportive and not waste your time with that loser!'

Lauretta was really upset, but would not back down. 'I'll show you, she said, he *will* get a job and *will* support me, oh, and by the way, I love him!'

David met Lauretta, at the Bear Public House, in Esher that evening; he could see she was upset and knew that she had been arguing with her father, so they found a quiet table at the rear of the bar and spoke. 'He is angry about you not working, said Lauretta, he thinks you will want me to support you, but I told him that you will get a job; that way, he will understand that you are capable of supporting me! Sorry darling, but I need to get him on my side; he owns my business, so if he wants too, he will sell it, and I don't want that.'

'I will get a job, I promise, replied David. It's my fault for being so bloody lazy, so I promise you, I will start looking! Anyway, are you still ok for next weekend, to meet my parents, they keep asking when they are going to meet you!'

Lauretta confirmed, that she couldn't wait to meet them.

David found a job, a week after their date at the Bear Pub in Esher, and became a trainee Travel Agent, for a small agency in Fetcham, Surrey.

Although the salary was not too bad, it would increase, once he had proved himself, to his new employers, but the job also had some "perks", with possible trips to various countries, which he would be expected to visit, to familiarise his knowledge of the areas, and would then be in a position to sell these to his clients.

He met Lauretta that evening, after his first day at his new job; she was so happy for him and said she would give it a few weeks, before she spoke to her father, as she knew he would probably say it wouldn't last.

David loved his job; he had now been there for over 3-months and had already earned some commission.

Lauretta spoke to her parents one evening, over dinner and mentioned that David was doing well with his new job at the Travel Agency and had already started to earn some commission, on top of his salary.

'Hmm, said Gregg Arnold, in response. We shall see!' *'Nothing I say will satisfy him,* Lauretta thought to herself!'

After his trial period of 6-months, David was given a contract of Employment by his company and a slight raise in his monthly salary, and couldn't wait to speak to Lauretta.

David had to work on the odd Saturday, at the Travel Agency, and being employed for a 5-day working week, would be allowed to have a day off, during the week. He arranged to take Lauretta out for lunch, close to her business in Margaret Street and arrived there early, then went inside, to surprise her.

He overheard a heated conversation between Lauretta and her father, coming from her office. He heard her say that she loved him, and would marry him and would also have his children, if he wanted them.

David walked back out to Margaret Street and wondered what it would take, for Lauretta's father to accept him, but for now, he would keep quiet.

Over lunch, David didn't say anything about overhearing the argument. He then grabbed both her hands, and whispered into her ear; 'I love you, Lauretta!'

The owner of the Travel Agency called David into his office. 'Please take a seat David, he said. I just wanted to congratulate you on your results, since you have worked here, over the past 8-months and we wanted to offer you a "Familiarisation Trip", which is coming up soon and also, as a bonus, you can take your partner with you.'

'I cannot thank you enough Mr Burton, I really love this job and a trip away is just what I needed. Thank you so much!'

'Our pleasure David and please, call me Paul; I will arrange the travel documents from the Tour Operator, and will get some dates back to you soon; just make sure your passport is in order, as you will be going to Spain!'

In all the excitement, David forgot to mention that he didn't have a passport, but knew that the agency had a courier service, who would deal with this. He telephoned them and asked what details were required, and they said they would pick up the documents, once he had completed them and would then take them to the London Passport office for him.

Lauretta was over the moon. '*We are going to Spain*, she shouted; and we're going together! A celebratory drink is called for she said, but first, I need a kiss!'

David told his parents, Constance and Charles, of his

trip to Spain, and that he would take Lauretta with him.

'We are so happy for you son, said his mother, and great news that Lauretta can go with you; she is such a lovely girl and we enjoyed her company, when she came for dinner. You must bring her over again soon.'

Lauretta gave the good news about her trip to Spain with David, to her parents, and her mother was so pleased for her; Gregg Arnold was not happy. 'So, you're still seeing that loser, he said. Alright, so he has a job, but I still say that he is a loser!'

'Daddy, please accept the fact that I love David, and want to be with him for the rest of my life and who knows, you may even become a grandfather one day!'

'Not with that loser, he said, when will you understand, I do *not* like him!'

Jennifer Arnold was seething. 'How dare you, she said, how dare you make our daughter unhappy, when she has found someone who loves her, how dare you!'

Lauretta and David arrived at Teruel Airport and took a taxi to the old town, where the tour operator had booked the hotel for them, for their 4-night stay.

On their first day, they were given a guided tour of the city, and David started writing down notes and taking photos of the churches and Cathedrals.

The following day, they were taken to the church of San Pedro, where they saw the two sarcophaguses of Isabela and Diego. The tour guide suggested that Lauretta "google" the tragic story, so that they could read the lengthy details of the tragedy.

The remainder of their trip was filled with further visits to churches, monuments and other historic places.

On their final evening, at a nearby restaurant, David proposed to Lauretta and she accepted.

'Just need to get daddy to come round,' she thought to herself!'

Lauretta had spoken to her parents, and had invited David over for lunch, after their return from Spain. She wondered how her father would react, then just before lunch was served, Gregg asked David to join him in his study, and gave him a beer.

'Well son, said Gregg, I understand you want to marry my daughter; ok, I agree to this, but there is something you must do first, before I give you both, my blessing!'

David was shocked at first, then realised that there must be a catch!

'If you can prove to me, within one year, that you can earn enough money to support my daughter, then I will allow you both to get married. I cannot be fairer than that, do you agree?'

During lunch, David didn't speak about Gregg's lecture, and although he joined in with the conversation, his mind was focused on his promise to Lauretta's father, knowing that he would have to earn enough money, within a 12-month period.

Lauretta could see that David's mind was in another place, but waited until after dinner, to discuss what her father had said to him.

'**What!** Shouted Lauretta. Now he *is* being unreasonable; how dare he dictate to you, David, about what he wants, what about me?'

Lauretta was about to confront her father, but David

asked her not to make things any worse.

'I will show him, said David. I will search for another job and I *will* earn enough money to support you!'

A week later, David had attended an interview for a new job, working in Corporate Travel, which would earn him four times the salary he was currently getting from the Travel Agency; the prospects were great, there was also a bonus scheme, and he couldn't wait to start.

David was given the position and had arranged to have dinner with Lauretta, that evening, at the "Hare and Hounds" pub, in Claygate, close to Esher. He tried to think of a way of breaking the news gently to Lauretta, but although everything sounded good, there was one major problem; the job was based in Miami, Florida!

David gave the details of the new position and Lauretta was so happy for him, but then he dropped the bombshell!

Lauretta banged her fist on the table, causing the other people in the pub to glance over, at the couple. 'This is all my father's fault, she said. I will confront him and sort this out, once and for all!'

Lauretta was unable to change her father's decision, even after threatening to leave, but after being told that she would lose her business, and get no funds from her family, she backed down.

David had given his two-week's notice at the Travel Agency and was ready to start his new employment, in Miami. Lauretta tearfully kissed him goodbye, after dropping him off at Heathrow Airport. David promised he would keep in touch as often as he could, and in one year from now, would be back, to speak to her father.

Lauretta really missed David's company, the trips to the pub, the restaurants and the love that he gave her.

After a month, contact between them was now minimal, and she wondered whether he had found someone else.

David was a success, in his new position.; he worked over 12-hours a day, and was taken out to the best restaurants in Miami, by his new employers, but all he wanted to do after work and dinner, was sleep!

Lauretta had been seeing an old boyfriend, not knowing that her father had set things up, but she only wanted someone to talk to, and have a drink with, and nothing else. She had tried several times to contact David, but each time, his voicemail kicked in. David sent her the odd email, and said he was missing her, but that his work schedule, and entertaining clients, gave him little time to speak.

It was almost a year since David had taken his new job in Florida, and Lauretta hoped he would call, or send a message, to say he would be home but she heard nothing!

David was offered a further year's contract, and a salary increase, from his American employers, which he accepted, but only subject to certain terms. He confirmed that he wanted to return to the UK, so that he could marry his girlfriend, and also told them that he would ask her to move to Florida.

They agreed to his terms, but asked him, if he could complete the big contract he was working on, with a Middle-Eastern Company, and tie it up, before he left for England.

It was 14-months ago, since David left for America, he had won the Middle-Eastern contract, and was given a Business-class, return ticket to Heathrow, and a £15k bonus, for his hard work, and he decided to surprise Lauretta, rather than call her.

David arrived at the 8-bedroomed house in Cobham, he had a large bunch of flowers behind his back, and had booked a table, at the Ivy, in Cobham Town Centre.

Jennifer Arnold, Lauretta's mother, opened the door, and was surprised to see him standing there.

'You had better come in, said Jennifer, don't worry, my husband is playing golf, and won't be back till later this evening!'

David sat down and was offered a drink, which he declined. 'Lauretta is out with friends, said Jennifer, she has been very upset over the lack of communication from you, so she has been dating an old boyfriend!'

David explained that he'd been working long hours, and had to achieve targets, which involved entertaining. 'Everything I did, said David, was to prove my love for your daughter, and I have done what your husband asked me to do; and I am now earning enough, to support Lauretta!'

David was starting to feel slightly upset, thinking that he had lost his love forever, but asked Jennifer to confirm their discussion to Lauretta, then placed the flowers on the table, and thanked Jennifer for her time, as he was leaving.

David rang Lauretta every day, hoping that her mother had explained the situation, but she didn't answer, or return his calls.

Two-months later, David's mother saw Lauretta in

Kingston, as she held hands with her boyfriend. Constance called out to Lauretta and gave her a kiss on the cheek; she said that David really misses her, and was sorry for the lack of contact from him. Lauretta explained that she had waited for his calls, but they never came. Then Constance saw a ring on her finger.

'This is my fiancé Simon, said Lauretta and we are due to be married, in 2-weeks-time.'

Constance wished them good luck and happiness, for their future together' she was upset, but could understand why her relationship with her son had failed.

David was distraught, when his mother confirmed that she had met Lauretta and her fiancé in Kingston, so he stormed out of the house, and ran all the way to his local pub, where he drank several pints of lager and a couple of whiskies, but knew this wouldn't help his predicament.

The drinking became a regular event, and he decided not to return to Florida, so he spent most of his time sleeping, and being a nuisance around his parent's house.

Lauretta married Simon as planned; the service was carried out at the Cobham United Church and was attended by over 100 people. The guests made their way to the Cobham Rugby Club, after the service; the same venue Lauretta had met David, on her 21st Birthday.

After dinner, the DJ played some background music; Lauretta remembered the Mike Oldfield, Incantations track, that David had played, at her Birthday party. She then looked across at the DJ and sighed; it wasn't David, but having learned of his success, knew that it wasn't him.

David's drinking became worse, he'd spent most of his money at the pub, or the local off-licence, and was going downhill very fast. His parents couldn't change his habits, but told him that he was only making things worse, due to constantly being drunk!

David had been drinking with an old friend, at a pub in Cobham, and his friend suggested he slow down, but David chose not to listen to him. He walked unsteadily, towards the road where Lauretta lived, with her parents, but didn't know if she was still living there, or had moved to a new house, with her new husband. He wanted to give Gregg Arnold a piece of his mind, and maybe more. He walked up to the door and rang the bell. Jennifer Arnold appeared. 'David, so good to see you, but why are you here?'

David started slurring his words and then shouted out, asking that he wanted to see Lauretta. Then she appeared, and he suddenly seemed to become sober, and looked at her, then tears started to flow.

'I love you Lauretta, come back to me, I did what I was asked to do, and you go off and marry someone else!'

Lauretta was upset, seeing David in this state, but told him that she was now happily married, and would be moving into a new house, very soon. 'Just one more kiss Lauretta; please, just one more!'

David collapsed on the doorstep, Lauretta called her mother, asking her to call an ambulance.

The ambulance arrived and pronounced that David had suffered a Heart-Attack and had died.

At the service, held at the All-Saints Church in Kingston; David had an "Open-Casket" Funeral.

After the service, his parents and relatives queued, to take a last look at his body and pay their respects.

Lauretta attended the funeral alone, and was quite upset. She looked at the queue of people, and after a few minutes, she ran over to the body of her former boyfriend, lying in the coffin, then bent over and kissed him on his cold lips. Her emotions took over; she wept noisily and shouted 'What have I done?' Lauretta fell back and landed on the floor. The vicar asked someone to call an ambulance, then bent over, to check on her condition, but Lauretta wasn't breathing!

Gregg and Jennifer Arnold attended the funeral of their beloved daughter Lauretta, who was diagnosed with "Stress-induced" Cardiomyopathy, which is better known as dying from a broken heart!

Jennifer Arnold started to look through her late daughter's belongings, and found some letters that David had written, 2 tickets from the Odeon Leicester Square, and a business card from the "Dishoom" Indian Restaurant, near Covent Garden. She cried when she saw these items, and knew that her daughter really loved David.

She then checked the photos on her daughters iPhone, and saw the pictures of the cathedrals and the church in San Pedro, showing the two sarcophaguses of Isabela and Diego. She also found a saved download on the mobile, and noticed it was about the San Pedro Church, so she sent it to her printer, and collected the 2 sheets of paper from it.

Jennifer started reading the story and started to cry, as it started to resemble similar occurrences, for her daughter, and her then boyfriend, David.

"In the Catalonian region of North-Eastern Spain, is the port-city of Tarragona. On the outskirts of the city, on higher ground and to the south of Aragon, is the city called Teruel. The city contains many monuments, churches and history.

The area also has many legends, thanks mainly to the famous story of the "Lovers of Teruel".

In a chapel, in the church of San Pedro, the legend states, that in the 13th Century, young Diego and Isabel died, because of an impossible love affair. The chapel contains a sarcophagus, for each of the lovers, which holds their mummified bodies. The story of how they fell in love and the reasons why their bodies lay "side by side", were written and kept in the church archives.

Jennifer continued to read.

"A long time ago, in the 1200's, in the city of Teruel, lived a young woman called Isabel, whose family were very rich. Isabel met a young man named Diego, who came from a poor family.

Isabel didn't care and they fell in love and wanted to marry. When Isabel told her parents, of her love for Diego, her parents said that they would not allow the marriage, as he didn't have enough money. When she told Diego, he told her not to worry and that if you wait for five years, I will earn enough money and then your parents will give me their consent.

Diego left Teruel, to find a job.

Isabel waited for a long time. Many men asked for her hand in marriage, but she refused. After five years, Diego had not returned and Isabel had not heard from him. Isabel's father wanted her to marry and finally, she agreed to marry another man.

The very next day after Isabel got married, Diego returned. Now, he had a lot of money. He was excited to see Isabel again and to finally marry her. But when he heard that Isabel was already married to another man, he was devastated.

That night, Diego went to Isabel's house. Isabel was inside her house with her new husband. Diego knocked on the door, and Isabel opened the door.
Diego said to Isabel, 'Give me a kiss, my love!'
Isabel said, 'No, I can't kiss you. I'm married.'
Diego replied. 'Please give me a kiss. If you don't kiss me, I'll die!'

Isabel insisted that she couldn't give him a kiss. And then, at that moment, Diego fell down and died right at Isabel's feet.

A few days later, at Diego's funeral, Isabel felt very bad because she hadn't kissed Diego when he asked her to. She decided to kiss Diego now. She jumped up out of her seat in the church and ran to his dead body, and she gave him a kiss. She kissed him so hard and so passionately that she died.

Finally, Isabel's parents understood the love between Isabel and Diego. They decided to bury the two bodies together, lying next to each other in the ground".

Jennifer couldn't stop crying and vowed to make things right, for her late daughter, so she contacted the churches, where each of the burials took place. She also contacted David's parents, and a week later, both the coffins, were buried side by side, in one grave.

3: NEXT STOP, BORDEAUX!

The 4 x 4 white Toyota Land Cruiser had boarded the Euro-shuttle, at Folkestone. The train was on time, as usual, and within minutes, the loudspeaker announced that the journey would take 35 minutes, to complete the journey, and arrive in Calais, France, then the train departed, and entered the Eurotunnel, bound for Calais.

Richard and Judith Colson, had driven from Epsom, Surrey, and took the M25, then the M20, to join the "Eurotunnel", for the start of their annual trip to France. They had travelled to most places in France, but this year, they had "mapped-out" the route to the southern parts, for a change. They had not pre-booked any accommodation, due to the time of year, with no school half-terms, or Bank Holidays, and were hopeful that they would find somewhere, in, or just outside the towns, on their journey, during their 2-week vacation.

They found the A16 road, which would take them down the east side of France, as they didn't want to drive via Paris, due to the additional time it would add to their journey.

The built-in Satnav, directed them to their first stop in

Alencon, not far from the famous area of Le Mans.

Judith managed to secure a room for the night, in an Ibis Hotel, inclusive of dinner. After a shower and change of clothes, they went down to the bar and ordered some drinks, before dinner. Richards Kronenbourg lager went down well, and Judith's Gin and Tonic, also "ticked" all the boxes!

They both ordered the Filet Mignon, together with a bottle of Malbec red wine, which complimented the medium-rare steaks.

Next morning, the Satnav took them on the road to La Rochelle, on the south-west coast, and on the Bay of Biscay; the drive took them nearly four hours, but when they arrived, the breath-taking views, made it all worth the long journey. They checked into the Hotel Champlain, in the town centre, and decided to stay for 2-nights, due to the stunning scenery and amount of seafood restaurants, they saw advertised, in the hotel reception.

Over the course of the next two days, they had taken a boat trip, from the harbour, which took them to Fort Boyard, and a stroll across the wonderful sandy beaches. They also hired some bicycles, so that they could see the magnificent landscapes, and the amazing amount of seafood restaurants, overlooking the Atlantic Ocean, made them want to spend some more time there.

That evening, they walked down to the harbour. It was thriving, with tourists, buskers and market stalls, all of which created a general lively atmosphere.

'Next stop Bordeaux, announced Richard!' They left the beautiful La Rochelle town after a casual breakfast, and headed back to the roads, where they would take the

2-hour journey, to their next destination.

In Bordeaux, they checked into the Novotel, which was in the centre and just a 5-minute walk into the old-town, so Richard left Judith to check-in, once reception gave him the details for parking, in the underground garage.

Richard found a suitable spot to park and, as he was reversing in, a tatty old yellow Citroën DS, tooted and gave him a rude gesture. Richard continued reversing, but the driver of the Citroën was shouting and swearing. Richard looked around, but couldn't understand what he had done wrong, so he got out of his car and walked over to the other car.

'Do you speak English, said Richard to the driver, is there a problem here?'

The Citroen driver backed away, then departed the garage, at high speed, leaving skid marks and smoke, coming from his tyres!

Richard joined his wife back in reception, he didn't mention the incident to her, or the Concierge, who had probably seen something, on his closed-circuit television screen.

After unpacking and walking into the old town, they admired the architecture of the Grand Theatre; the Sante-Croix church and the medieval wall, around Place de la Bourse.

Time flew by so quickly, so they looked for a place to have dinner. The weather was quite warm and they spotted some outside seating, at Le Petit Commerce, a small bistro, but Richard seemed to recall Rick Stein having eaten there, in one of his weekend-away programmes. They shared some Moules Mariniere to start, followed by Filet-Mignon, complimented by a bottle of St Emilion. As they ate, Richard looked at some people standing outside the restaurant and realised they were waiting for a table; he remarked to Judith about how popular this bistro was. He then spotted the owner of the Citroën car; he had seen earlier in the underground car park, but didn't want to confront him, so he looked the opposite way.

'Monsieur, said the waiter, are you ready for some dessert?' Richard confirmed that they had finished and asked for the bill.

'L'addition, s'il vous plait?' said Richard.

The waiter gave them the bill and thanked them for their custom. As soon as they left their seats, a man pushed past them, and nearly knocked Judith over; then Richard saw that it was the man from the underground garage. 'Why are you being so rude, asked Richard; and what was that all about in the car park?'

The man looked at Richard and muttered something, then waved his hands at him, as if to say "go away"!

Judith asked her husband about the incident, when they walked back to their hotel, so Richard explained about the incident in the car park and couldn't understand what he had done?

'Never mind darling, said Judith, we are leaving here tomorrow morning, so let's forget about it!'

After checking out of the hotel, they went in to the car park, where Richard checked their car, to make sure there was no damage and couldn't see anything. They checked the map and placed the destination details into the satnav. The roads were quiet, when they left the old town of Bordeaux; the satnav confirmed that their journey time would be 2-3 hours, before they would arrive in Toulouse.

They found the Mercure Hotel, in Toulouse town centre and checked in; the underground car park was quite full, but Richard managed to find a vacant space. He found Judith at the reception desk, and the porter took their bags up to their room. Richard had to go back to the car, he'd left his mobile on the charger, so he left Judith to unpack and took the lift to the car park.

He found his car and took out his mobile, when he heard a car horn beeping; he looked across and saw the tatty old yellow Citroën DS. *'Surely he hasn't followed us all the way from Bordeaux,'* he thought?

He walked over to the Citroën, to see if it was the same man, but the car reversed, and sped off towards the ramp. Richard managed to get a photo of the registration and wondered whether to alert the police, but thought about it, knowing that no crime had been committed.

Judith wanted to check out some of the art galleries and museums, so they had a light lunch in a bistro, close to the main square; the Place du Capitole.

The rest of the day was spent looking at the magnificent architecture and more museums, including the Musée des Augustins.

As they wandered back to the hotel, Richard thought again, about the yellow Citroen and wondered if they were being stalked. He didn't want to mention to Judith, that he had seen the car in the hotel garage and decided to keep it to himself.

The following morning, they checked out of the Mercure Hotel; Judith wanted to stay another night, but Richard made a feeble excuse about how packed the place was and that they would be able to relax, once they had reached their next place.

In the underground garage, Richard looked around, to see if the Citroën was parked there, and was glad he couldn't see the car, and came to the conclusion that the whole situation was just a coincidence.

Judith checked the map, and asked Richard if he had thought about the next stage of their journey, so he suggested that she closed her eyes, and waggle her finger over the map and that would be the next stop.

Judith's finger landed on a place called Millau. Richard entered the details into the satnav, and saw that the journey would take them just over a couple of hours.

'So, Millau it is then,' said Richard!

The traffic was quite heavy, but they soon entered the N88 road; Richard kept looking in his rear-view mirror, to see if they were being followed, but couldn't see a tatty yellow Citroen behind them.

Judith started to read her guide book, to see what was in Millau, and mentioned to Richard that there was a huge viaduct, which was used by traffic, coming from Paris, heading for Montpelier, of which Norman Foster Architects, were involved in the planning. 'Really,' said Richard, with an uninterested look on his face!

They saw the magnificent Millau viaduct in the distance, with its seven cable-stays and seven pylons; Judith then confirmed that the bridge was over 8,000 feet in length, and had a height of over 1,000 feet.

They found an Ibis hotel in the town centre and parked their car, in an adjoining car park. After a quick freshen-up, they strolled into the town and found a small bistro, but the menu contained only contained eight items, so they chose the cassoulet, which they thoroughly enjoyed, washed down with a glass each, of Côtes du Roussillon.

The sun was getting warmer, and Richard wished that Judith had picked somewhere by the sea. They wandered away from the small bistro, and found another museum, but as it was quite small, so Richard stayed outside; his mind was on other things, and he couldn't stop thinking about the Citroen and its owner!

Richard fancied a cool beer, due to the temperature rising rapidly; they found a small bar, close to the town centre and sat below a large umbrella, which advertised Kronenbourg, but didn't sell it. They settled for two ice-cold bottles of Stella Artois, which Richard announced came from Belgium, not France, then Judith asked him if he was getting bored, due to his corny jokes and constantly looking over his shoulder, but he offered no response.

The evening was a lot cooler and they noticed that all the restaurants had queues outside. They ended up in an Italian restaurant, but found the food exceptionally good, as they sat outside and "People Watched", before their meal was served. Judith commented on the "chic" French fashion, for both the men and the women, but. Richard was trying to catch the waiter's attention, to get some more beers.

They had just finished their meal, when they heard a commotion going on, close by; two men were arguing about something, which involved the owner of the Italian restaurant to intervene.

Judith glanced at the two men, who looked as if they were about to exchange blows, but the Italian restaurant owner managed to pull them apart and offered them each a drink, to cool things down.

The men walked away, in different directions, without accepting the drink, but everyone was relieved, when the argument was over. 'Wonder what that was all about,' said Richard?

'Not sure, said Judith, but I seem to recognise one of them, as being in Bordeaux; you remember Richard, the rude one, who nearly knocked me over, in the restaurant!'

The colour started to disappear from Richard's face; all he could think of, was that this man had followed them from Bordeaux, then from Toulouse, but why?

Judith knew Richard was not his normal self, and asked him what the problem was. He explained that he had seen the Citroen again, in Toulouse and that it was possible he had followed them to Millau.

'That's it, said Judith, we're going to the police!'

Richard stated that the man had committed no crime against them, and it could just be a coincidence that he had turned up in Millau.

'Anyway, said Richard, we can't let this spoil our French Trip, where are we going next?'

'Darling, said Judith, I know it's a long way from here, but why don't we take the road over the viaduct, towards Paris?'

'Great idea, said Richard, we can always stop somewhere along the way!'

They checked out the next morning and took their overnight bags back to the car. Judith shouted '*NO*!' A deep scratch had been gouged onto both the passenger side doors. Richard checked the rest of the car ,and saw the word "Meurtier", scratched onto the boot.

Richard shouted, and asked Judith to get in the car quickly; they left Millau, and followed the signs to the viaduct and the route to Paris. Judith had been quiet, but suddenly asked what this was all about and what the word means. 'It translates to murderer, confirmed Richard, this maniac must be mistaking me for someone else and has been following us; so, we're taking no chances!'

They had just entered the viaduct, when they saw the tatty yellow Citroën DS ; the car passed them at great speed, then it indicated, to join their lane, it then slowed down, until their Toyota was right behind it.

Richard indicated and pulled into the left-hand lane, just in front of the Citroen, which then accelerated and once again, pulled out ahead of them. 'I'm calling the police,' shouted Judith! Richard pulled out, and put this foot hard down on the accelerator, until he was going over 80mph.

The Citroen caught up with Richard's car, and "tailgated" him for a brief moment, but Richard upped his speed to 90mph, then 100mph!

The Citroen caught up once more, but this time, Richard slammed his brakes down, hard! The Citroen crashed into the rear of the Toyota, causing both its airbags to inflate, and spin the car round several times.

The Citroen veered off to the right, with flames appearing and then became airborne, everything seemed to be moving in slow motion. It went through the gap, and plummeted the 1000 feet, then exploded, just before it landed in the river Tarn, below.

The Police Nationale, and the Gendarmes arrived, followed by two ambulances. The paramedics made sure that Richard and Judith were not injured, but they confirmed that they were just badly shaken, by the crash, and the exploding airbags.

Richard had asked Judith not to mention anything about the man in the Citroen, as a police officer with a notepad, walked towards them. The police officer took their statements, and checked their documentation, then confirmed that their vehicle would be towed away to a local garage.

'The ambulance took them to hospital, after seeing a few bruises appearing, so that they could be fully checked over. They were released after an hour; then a nurse called a taxi, to take them back to Millau.

They checked back into the same Ibis hotel in the town, and asked the concierge to contact the local police, to confirm where they were staying.

A police officer arrived the following morning and asked them a few more questions, and mentioned the word "Meurtier", that was scratched onto the boot and asked if Richard could explain. Richard shrugged his shoulders, and said he hadn't seen it. Judith said she had seen some deep scratches on the passenger side doors, but nothing else. 'Why officer,' asked Richard?

The officer explained that the man was known to the police in Bordeaux, and Toulouse and had been arrested a few times, for harassing people, but nothing like this! The officer further explained that the man had died from his injuries, and was probably dead, before his car landed into the river.

The 4 x 4 white Toyota Land Cruiser was a "write-off" and was left in France. The couple returned home to Epsom and took a few days off from work, to recuperate

after their ordeal and also, to make arrangements for a
new car, and other items, through their insurance
companies. All the paperwork was completed and they
received a hire car, until they had found a replacement,
for their written-off vehicle, in France.

Richard had ordered a new 4 x 4 white Toyota Land
Cruiser, which they both went to Purley, near Croydon,
to pick up.

The agent for the dealership thanked them for the
business, and gave them some coffee, while they waited
for their new car to be driven onto the forecourt. The
agent asked Richard about the damage they had repaired
on his last car, and hoped he was satisfied with the
service he was given, at the time.

On the way home, Judith asked Richard about the
damage, that the agent had mentioned, and explained
that he had a slight "shunt", about three-months ago,
when he was driving back from London.

Judith started to worry about the ordeal with the
yellow Citroen, which started to haunt her; she then
thought about why the man would follow them from
Bordeaux, then Toulouse and then Millau.

Richard went off to play golf with some friends, the
next morning; Judith had a bad night's sleep, and wanted
to check a few things on her computer.

She checked some newspapers online, and found an
unsolved fatality that had occurred about three-months
ago. She opened a drawer of the desk in the study, to
find Richard's diary, and checked to see if there were
any entries for three-months ago.

She went back to the computer and read about a
French woman, who was killed, by a "Hit and Run"

incident, in Clapham North, southwest London.

Richard's entry in the diary, for the same date read "London works meeting at 4pm, dinner at La Rueda, Tapas bar in Clapham North – OOOPS!"

4: THE TOWER OF TERROR

Jake Thorne and his best mate Steve Mellor, met in the All-Bar One Wine Bar, in Bedford Street, close to Covent Garden, in central London.

They both worked in Aldwych, for the same company, importing and exporting fashion accessories, all over the world. They didn't enjoy working for the company, but the wages were paid on time, at the end of each month.

They had a couple of beers each and decided to make their way to Charing Cross Railway Station, then London Bridge and finally, to Purley, where they lived quite close to each other.

Both Jake and Steve had girlfriends; Lorraine and Tania; they all got on well with each other and had decided to take a 2-week trip to California, to visit various resorts on the Pacific Coast Highway, and, for the final couple of days, to see the Theme-Parks in Anaheim.

It was a cold morning in Purley, Jakes father picked up the two couples around 6 am, and dropped them off at

West Croydon, ready for their approximate bus journey of 2 hours, to London Heathrow Airport.

The plane touched down at San Francisco Airport, after being in the air for just over 11 hours. Everyone was excited and ready for their "trip of a lifetime".

After handing their passports and visas for checking, they were given the directions for the Car Rental outlet, where they picked up a Toyota, which was large enough for the four of them and their luggage. They had landed at midnight, UK time, so they turned their watches back 8 hours, to coincide with the current Pacific Standard Time Zone.

Jake punched the details into the car's Satnav, which took them into the town centre, where they had booked the Handlery Hotel, in Union Square, for a 2-night stay. After the approximate 40-minute journey, their Car was taken from them, by the hotel's "Car Jockey", who delivered the keys back to them, while they checked in, at reception. Steve noticed the uniforms of the "Bell-Hops", which looked like something from an old Hollywood movie.

After unpacking their clothes and other items, they all met in the Hotel reception, where Jake had already discussed the best places to eat, with the Hotel Concierge.

Knowing everyone loved seafood, they took a taxi to "Fisherman's Wharf", where they were spoilt for choice, and, by the time they had sampled the wonderful Clam Chowder, En-route to the recommended restaurant, they found the "Fog Harbour Fish House", where the ambience, the food, and the service was first class.

Jake and Lorraine had managed to overcome the "Jet-

Lag", after a good night's sleep, and wandered around Union Square, to check out the shops. They spotted "Chinatown", not too far from the hotel and a Macy's store, also with walking distance. Lorraine was happy, as they walked arm in arm around the square, and Jake planted a "wet-smacker" onto Lorraine's cheek, so she cuddled into him, and asked if this was a dream.

Jake and Tania found the happy couple wandering back to the Handlery Hotel, and asked if they had eaten breakfast, so they found a Denny's Diner close by, where they ate a large portion of pancakes, eggs, bacon and grits.

Jake had arranged a trip across to Alcatraz, and a taxi took them to Pier 33, where they picked up the ferry. Steve noticed the clouds passing over, once they boarded the ferry and it rained all the way across the bay, leaving the sun behind them. Lorraine commented 'Spooky'!

The Rangers gave them the guided tour around Alcatraz Island, showing them the cell, where Clint Eastwood had filmed "Escape from Alcatraz". They also saw the cells where the "Birdman of Alcatraz", and Al Capone had been confined, for their crimes.

After landing back at Pier 33, the sun returned. Lorraine commented again, with her "Spooky" remark.

They all enjoyed their brief stay in San Francisco, and headed for the Pacific Highway, for the next stop, in Monterey, where they had booked 3-nights, at the Cannery Row Inn. They were amazed at the number of restaurants, and other attractions, that were once used for sardine canning and more famously, there was a book called "Cannery Row", by John Steinbeck.

'I feel it's theme park time,' said Jake. Everyone

agreed. 'Do you remember the fairground scenes for the movie "The Lost Boys", asked Jake, well that is where we are off to, we are going to Santa Cruz!'

The journey took them just over an hour, before thy arrived at the Santa Cruz Beach Boardwalk, and noticed straight away, the "Giant Dipper". They tried all the rides, including the carousel, where you picked up a ring and threw it into the mouth of a clown.

On their way back to their hotel, they stopped in Carmel, where Clint Eastwood was once the mayor. 'Awesome, commented Lorraine!

'Next stop Pismo Beach, said Jake, time to top up the tan!'

Their journey also included Santa Monica, Santa Barbara, and a trip into Los Angeles, before the final stop, at the Holiday Inn, in Anaheim, for the last three days of their holiday. 'It's going far too quickly, said Lorraine.'

'Agreed said Tania!' After breakfast, they boarded a bus, which took them to Knotts-Berry Farm, which they learned, was the site that Walt Disney wanted to buy, for his first Disneyland Theme Park, in 1955, but he was not successful.

They all enjoyed the "Silver Bullet" Steel Roller Coaster, the "Ghost Rider", which is the longest wooden roller coaster, on the west coast, and the side shows. They moved on and had to queue for 20 minutes, but finally, they boarded the amazing, "Xcelerator" Roller Coaster, which took their breath away, literally!

Their final day was spent in Disneyland, which was quite busy. Jake spotted the "Twilight Zone, Tower of Terror" and noticed that the queue was quite short.

'What's this all about,' asked Tania?

Jake had heard about the ride, which transported the passengers in an Elevator, up to approximately 180 feet, then dropped the Lift in "Free-Fall", which would result in screams and nervous clapping, from the unsuspecting riders, unless it was their second or third time.

As they entered the building, which was based on the fictional Hollywood Tower Hotel, they were greeted by a "Bell-Hop". Lorraine commented on the striking resemblance to the Bell-Hops at the Handlery, in San Francisco.

They entered a square shaped vehicle and the restraint bars were pushed over their bodies. As they moved slowly forward, the theme from the Twilight Zone started playing and the voice of Rod Serling (The original presenter of the Twilight Zone TV series) began to narrate the story, of the ill-fated hotel, which was struck by lightning in 1939, causing the guest elevator, part of the structure, and several guests to mysteriously vanish. 'Spooky' again,' said Lorraine!

The car slowly twisted and turned on its track, then swivelled, and faced a large mirror – Five ghostly figures appeared, causing some of the female occupants to scream. It then swivelled back into place and continued along the dark passageway, then through a large set of powered lift doors. The car clicked into place and the doors automatically closed; there was silence, everyone wondered what was about to happen next!

"*Whoosh*"! The car shot vertically upwards, inside the dark shaft, at great speed, then the elevator doors opened, revealing a magnificent view of the theme park. The doors then closed, and the elevator dropped, at full speed, and you could hear the screams all over Disneyland!

The car suddenly stopped, sighs of relief were heard, but then, it shot up the dark shaft once more, again to even more screams; the doors once again, opened up and closed once more, and this time, you could hear, 'Oh no, not again, please, no more'! Then it dropped again.

The car unhitched itself and started to make its way back along the tracks. At the end of the track, the restraints were lifted, the passengers left the ride and were ushered to a gift shop, where you could purchase photos of the riders, all looking visibly shocked and frightened.

A young girl, who worked in the ride's Gift shop, had laid out two sets of photos. She looked carefully at the first set of photos, then the second set, which were taken on the two drops, and contacted a colleague.

The colleague checked the photo of two couples, who sat at the rear of the ride, on the initial drop, but were not on the photo of the second drop.

The ride manager was called, who then telephoned the ride supervisor, and asked what number of persons had ridden in car number 4, on the previous journey. 'There were 44 persons on that journey, said the supervisor, why?'

The manager contacted the Orange County police, to confirm that 44 persons had ridden the Tower of Terror ride, and that only 40 persons had returned.

After weeks of investigations, a press release confirmed that four persons had gone missing, during a ride on the Tower of Terror attraction, at the Disneyland theme Park, in Anaheim, California. The names of the missing persons were Jake Thorne, Stephen Mellor, Lorraine Carter and Tania Williams, all from Purley, in Surrey, England.

It was also confirmed that no bodies had been found, and the Orange County Police Department, are undertaking a detailed search; therefore, the ride has been temporarily closed, until further notice.

An Elevator Consultant had checked the ride from top to bottom, and had also seen the photos of the first and second drops. He reported that he could find no evidence of mechanical or electrical failure and the ride, in his opinion, was therefore, safe to use.

13 years later, at the Disneyland Theme Park in Anaheim, California, the Tower of Terror ride was still attracting people from all over the world. The car followed the tracks, and eventually clipped into place. The elevator doors closed and the car shot vertically upwards. It repeated the manoeuvre three times, as the park managers were trying to attract more passengers, by occasionally changing the number of drops.

Forty people entered the car at the start of the ride, but forty-four people departed the car, when it finished.

The girl in the gift shop laid out all the photos, for each of the three drops, and noticed that four, additional persons had appeared, on the third drop.

The ride manager was called, the Orange County Police were called, and more investigations were undertaken.

The two couples were questioned at the local Police Station, and each gave the same story, stating that they had been on the "Tower of Terror" ride and that they had been on a 2-week holiday in California; and tomorrow, would be returning home, to the UK. 'Why do you ask, have we done something wrong,' said Jake?

'What year is this,' asked the Police lieutenant?

Lorraine gave the officer a quizzical look. 'What is going on here, asked Steve?

'The four of you, entered the Tower of Terror ride, on the 21st March 2009, stated the lieutenant, is that correct?'

All four of them looked at the officer, then Jake asked again, if they had done something wrong.

'No crime has been committed here, said the officer, but I have to confirm something that may come as a shock!'

'Today, is the 21st March, 2022!'

5: THE TATTOOIST

Balham High Road, in South-west London, was busy as usual, with potential shoppers who lived local, either queuing in the Boots Chemist, or buying a paper, a book, or stationary, at WH Smiths.

The small shop, quite close to Balham underground station had a "Let Agreed" notice, recently fitted. Many of the local people peered through the shop front, to try and get an idea of what the shop would become. The shop also included a one-bedroomed flat, directly above, which made the new lessee had made, a requirement.

Rod Grainger was born in Oldridge Road, Balham, SW12, not too far from the High Road. His parents had owned a grocers shop close by, but had both passed away, just over a year ago, from natural causes, mainly due their ages and ongoing ill health.

Rod inherited several thousand pounds, after his parent's wills had been certified. He was an only child and was born in 1980, but he missed a lot of his schooldays, due to not being concerned about his education, except for the Art classes, which he never missed. Rod made a living buying and selling goods, that were either broken and fixable, or purchased from eBay and sold at a higher price, which worked sometimes, but not always.

He was always taking chances, betting on outsiders, in horse racing, or football matches.

Rod had only a few friends, but his best mate, Brian, who had owned a Tattoo parlour in Tooting Broadway, had just passed away, due to an overdose of drugs and heavy drinking.

The Tattoo parlour closed down, then the shop was rented out, and became a Hairdressing Salon.

Rod was interested in becoming a qualified Tattoo artist, and with the cash he had just inherited, he signed the paperwork, for the rental of the shop in Balham.

He paid for the interior decoration, the machines, the sterilising equipment and the ink stock, and he named the shop "Tattoo", a simple name, but *he* liked it.

Rod had advertised in the local paper, the Wandsworth Guardian, and was surprised with the amount of interested applicants who applied for the position.

At the interviews, he wanted to take on a qualified tattooist, who would have the time to train Rod, with the unique skills, he would need.

The preferred candidate was a Turkish man from Streatham, named Sinan, who was very qualified and would bring customers in, from his last business in Croydon, which was closed down, due to a proposed new shopping centre being built, close to the shop he rented there.

Prior to the opening day, Sinan had taught Rod the basic skills he would require, and was confident that his new boss would soon be able to become a competent Tattooist, maybe within a month, or two.

The shop opened and a few people entered the parlour. A young girl, who looked under age, but confirmed she was eighteen, asked if she could have a small butterfly tattooed onto her shoulder.

An old client of his late, best mate Brian, entered the shop and shook Rod's hand, and he browsed through the design catalogue, and chose to have a small eagle inked on to his right arm.

Other customers chose designs, including "Love" and "Hate", in capital letters, on their knuckles; Dolphins on their arms or legs, and love hearts, with the name of their partners, on different parts of their bodies.

Rod was pleased with the interest for his new business; Sinan was equally happy that he was busy. The Appointment Diary was looking very healthy and Rod wondered whether he would need to take on additional help, but for now, he decided to wait for a month, based on a discussion with Sinan, who'd had previous experience.

It was 3-months later; Rod had become more confident that he could use his new skills, and become a Tattooist.

His first client was a young lady, who asked for an "Om" symbol, to be tattooed onto the back of her neck; Rod had heard about the powerful symbol before, which was regarded as one of the most sacred mantras, in the Hindu religion, being a combination of the spiritual, and the physical, and referring to life and the universe.

The lady was thrilled with the design, after Rod showed her, with the use of a mirror. Rod was happy with his first Tattoo and Sinan complimented him, on his very first design.

After 6-months, the Tattoo parlour was always very busy; Rod and Sinan had interviewed more potential candidates for the position, and after narrowing the number down to two, decided to take on a Spanish man called Santiago, who had owned a tattoo business in Madrid, but due to an acrimonious, and costly divorce settlement, came to England, to stay with his parents, in Streatham.

Everyone liked Santiago, he was friendly, he made the clients laugh, and his designs were very impressive, and he could tattoo any design, the clients wanted.

Sinan noticed that more and more of their clients were asking for tattoos relating to snakes, or dragon-like serpents; these designs also included flames, surrounding or just below the reptiles, with other designs showing two snakes, in an "S" shape, intertwined.

Sinan had seen similar tattoos a long time ago, but only one or two, so after work, he checked his old photographs, of the designs he had tattooed on clients, and found the intertwined design, which was taken 5 years ago, on a female customer.

He googled the design and eventually found what he was looking for; It was called "Sugaar", meaning "Serpent and Fire", and was a design used in the Basque regions of Spain.

Sinan read more about the "Sugaar", which revealed stories, about a snake that lived underground and would emerge from chasms or caves, near mountains. Also, there were stories of men and women, in various areas of the Basque regions, who worshipped the "Sugaar" and would perform rituals, that would make thunder and lightning, suddenly appear. He continued to read.

"According to a legend, two young men from Dima (Biscay) saw Sugaar in a cave in Baltzola. The youngest cut his tail by striking him with a stone; the oldest, on the contrary, disapproved of his brother's action. Some years later, the oldest brother was living far from home and, feeling homesick; he met a mysterious man who took him to the Baltzola Cave; all of a sudden.

When they said goodbye to each other, the mysterious man gave him a box full of gold for him, and a red belt for his younger brother. The youngest brother refused to wear it and fastened it to a chestnut tree. The tree was soon on fire and, later, only a hole remained. Then, both brothers noticed that the mysterious man was Sugaar.

'The next day, Sinan saw that Santiago was tattooing a pair of intertwined snakes, one on each arm, for a new client; Sinan wanted to ask Santiago about the design, but he was working on a crystal skull, which would take up the whole of the man's chest, just above his stomach.

Rod had been asked to provide a Tarot card, with "The Lovers", which was quite complex and revealed two skulls and flowers, onto the tarot card.

After work one evening, Rod invited his two colleagues upstairs to his flat, for a drink and a take-away, so that they could discuss the business, and also, to get some ideas of anything they should be doing, to ensure the business was going in the right direction.

They each had a cold beer and chinked their glasses, then Sinan suggested that they change the shop's name, from "Tattoo", to "Tattoo You", based on the Rolling Stones Album, from 1981.

'Great idea, said Rod, I will arrange it!'

Santiago asked Rod, if he could get some more artwork on the snake designs, as they seemed to be a very popular choice lately, from their customers.

'No problem, Iago, said Rod, these do seem to be going down well lately, let me order a brochure tomorrow, or see if I can download something online.'

Santiago preferred to be called Iago, but didn't like it, when Rod called Sinan, "Sin", for reasons he did not disclose.

The new sign was fitted 3-weeks later, Rod had registered the new business name at Companies House, and had arranged for a celebratory open-day, for existing and potential new clientele, offering some drinks and snacks and also, vouchers offering discounts, for new tattoos.

Sinan asked for a couple of days off, due to his parents coming to the UK from their home in Ankara, the Turkish capital, so Rod asked if he wanted more time, as it was his parents, but Sinan confirmed they were only here for a couple of days, and were off to Canada, to see his older brother, and their three grandchildren.

Iago worked harder, during the two days, Sinan had taken off, but he was happy doing what he liked and never complained.

A new customer came in and apologised that he had not booked an appointment, but Rod confirmed that they should be able to "squeeze" him in, in about an hour's time, subject to his requirements, and asked him what he would like.

The middle-aged man asked for the "Sugaar" intertwined snake design, together with flames below; and produced a photograph, detailing the exact design he wanted.

Iago overheard the conversation and asked Rod if he could carry out the tattoo for the man, as this design would probably take up to a week, to complete. Rod agreed and confirmed the cost to the man, who sat patiently, until he was called.

After 4 days and three-hours, the "Sugaar" design and flames, had been tattooed onto the entire width and length, of the man's back.

The tattoo was admired by the recipient, when a large mirror was produced by Rod. The customer stated that he would be showing his friends and hoped that the tattoo parlour would receive a lot more business.

Sinan returned a week later and apologised for taking additional days off, but stated that he had called several times, to confirm that his parents had both been quite ill, resulting in them both going to hospital. Rod was more worried about Sinan's parents, and asked if they had recovered. Sinan confirmed that they were still in hospital, undergoing various tests, as the doctors were unable to diagnose exactly what they were suffering from.

Sinan was amazed at the number of bookings the parlour had received and also, the number of people sitting and waiting for a tattoo.

The walls of the parlour were covered in photos of the tattoos given to their clientele, since the shop had opened. Sinan noticed the "Sugaar" and flames, and knew that this was one of Iago's, then he looked more closely, and thought he could see something moving on the design. *'Too many late nights,'* he thought!

The parlour was a roaring success, following referrals from satisfied clients, so Rod gave both Sinan and Iago a generous bonus, as a thank you, for their hard work.

Iago met some friends that evening, in the Manor Arms pub, in Mitcham Lane, Streatham, where they spoke about the tattoo parlour he worked at, and asked if he had recently carried out a "Sugaar" design, on someone's entire back. Iago confirmed that he had completed one recently, and one of his friends explained that they had recommended the parlour to someone, who would soon be joining their sect. Iago thanked them for the referrals, and offered them a discounted tattoo, when they wanted one.

Sinan watched Iago finishing another "Sugaar" tattoo, and saw some words on the man's back; he looked across and saw Iago showing the man the wording, with a mirror, and as he walked pass, he read the words, which he knew were Spanish. "Adorador de Serpientes".

Rod told his assistant's that he was shortly about to take a week's holiday with some friends, and that Sinan would be in charge, until he returned. They both told him that he deserved it, for all his hard work making the shop very successful, for all of them, and told him to enjoy himself.

Rod travelled to Bilbao, on a BA flight; he picked up a hire car at the airport and travelled the 70 miles to Donostia San Sebastian, to join his friends, for a stag night, a wedding, and then a few days after, to relax.

He checked into the Maria Cristina Hotel, later in the afternoon, then met a few of his friends in the downstairs bar, before getting ready to meet everyone, that evening.

The choice of tapas bars in the old town were endless, even though most of them were full, but Rob and three of his friends found a spare, outside table, at the "Bar la Viña" restaurant, due to some people confirming that they were about to leave, after settling their bill.

The tortilla, gambas and croquettas were all exceptional, as were the many glasses of "Cruz Campo" draught beers, or "Cerveza de Barril", as the Spanish waiter constantly called out.

The groom finally turned up, about an hour later, after Rod had contacted and told him where they were, so a few more Cervezas were ordered, and the drinking continued.

Only Rod and one of his friends made it to breakfast, the next morning, just ten-minutes before it was due to close and get ready for lunches. They both had hangovers, but after a few cups of coffee, and some pastries, they both felt *slightly* better and returned to their rooms, to get ready for the wedding.

The wedding was held at the Miramar Palace, in the heart of the city, where the views of the bay, and Santa Cara Island, made the venue special, for the new bride and groom.

Everybody was seated after the ceremony and Rod was split up from his friends, as the groom knew they could be quite boisterous, after a few too many beers.

Rod sat next to a Spanish man, who spoke very good English. The man, who introduced himself as Paco, asked Rod what he did for a living. When Rod told him he was a Tattooist, Paco rolled up one of his shirtsleeves and showed him his tattoo; it was two intertwined snakes, with flames below and the inscription below, which Rob recognised.

'Ah, said Rod, the "Sugaar"!'

Paco looked at Rod and asked him how he knew, and Rod explained that one of his tattooists, named Santiago, had been applying this and similar snake designs, on many of their customers.

'You should be very careful, stated Paco, the "Sugaar" tattoo could mean that these people belong to a "Snake, or Serpent" worship cult, and they would entice people into their places of worship, to participate in various rituals!'

Rod had never seen whether Iago had any tattoos, but changed the subject. 'So, Paco, do you live here in San Sebastian,' asked Rod?

Paco confirmed that he lived in Santander, which was just over 2-hours from here and approximately 200km. He also confirmed that his father was the uncle of the bride.

The whole evening went very well, Rod had been talking to a pretty Spanish girl called Maria-Jose. They both swapped numbers, after they had danced and cuddled, when the DJ played "Hero", by Enrique Iglesias.

Rod spent the last few days relaxing in San Sebastian; he contacted Maria-Jose and thanked her for her company at the wedding, and arranged to meet in Bilbao, the day he was due to return back to the UK, so that they could visit the Guggenheim Museum, and to have some lunch.

They kissed goodbye and promised they would keep in touch, then Maria-Jose said she was going over to see her aunt who lived in Chelsea, in four to six weeks, once she had arranged the time off, with her employers. 'Please can we meet up, when you come over,' asked Rod? Maria-Jose said she would text him, once she had the dates, and kissed him hard, on his lips. 'Thank you so much for making me very happy,' said Maria-Jose! 'My pleasure,' replied Rod!

Rod arrived at the tattoo parlour, the day after he returned from Spain. Sinan confirmed that everything was good, and that business was still on the increase. Iago had just finished with a client and asked Rod how the wedding went. Rod said it went very well, but didn't mention anything about his discussions with Paco, during the wedding.

Iago left the shop, just after finishing with a client, around 6.30pm, so Rod asked Sinan if he had 5-minutes for a chat. 'Is everything OK,' asked Sinan?

Rod told Sinan about his discussion with Paco, at the wedding, and wondered whether Iago was involved with a Snake-Worship Cult, but had never seen whether he had the "Sugaar" tattoo, on his body. 'Maybe we should take a visit to Streatham, said Sinan, we should arrange to meet up with him, one weekend and maybe, after a few beers, he might tell us a bit more about his interests?'

A fortnight later, the three of them had arranged to meet in the Greyhound pub, in Streatham. Iago said that it was good of them to travel to Streatham, but they said it was only a couple of stops on the train, and that he should come to Balham, next time.

They sat at a table in the bar and started talking about Rod's trip to Spain. 'So, said Iago, you have met a

Spanish senorita, my friend!'

Rod explained that Maria-Jose would be coming to England in a few weeks and would introduce her to them. They also spoke about Iago's parents and his business in Madrid, then about Sinan's parents. 'So, what do you do when you're not working Iago,' asked Rod?

Iago said that his normal weekend evenings were having a few beers with some Spanish friends and sometimes, the odd meeting, at a club, where he and other Spanish people, played music and watched movies. 'Sounds good said Sinan, maybe we could get an invitation sometime?'

Iago gave them both a casual glance, wondering what they were up to, but agreed that he would arrange something soon.

Rod asked if anyone fancied another pint of San-Miguel, but Iago confirmed it was his round. He left the table and dropped his keys, then, as he bent over to retrieve them, his t-shirt rose up, and revealed the "Sugaar" tattoo, across his back. Both Rod and Sinan caught a quick glimpse, but said nothing.

Maria-Jose arrived at Heathrow Airport and took the underground train to Earl's Court, then changed onto the district line, for one more stop, taking her to West Brompton. She walked along Brompton Road, then turned left into Redcliffe Gardens, where the properties were valued at £1million upwards.

Maria-Jose called Rod, and told her she would like to meet up sometime. Rod said he would have picked her up at the airport, but was happy she was safe and in the

UK.

Sinan had been doing some digging, hoping that he would find some details about snake worship, but couldn't find anything on social media. He had Iago's address, which was on file, at the tattoo parlour, so he travelled up to Streatham, to see if he could find out whether there were any halls or other places, in the vicinity, near Gleneagle Road, the address he jotted down, from the work files.

Sinan couldn't find anything in the actual road, so he made his way back to Streatham High Road, and stopped for a pint in a pub called the Bull, near the train station; it wasn't packed, and he was served by a young lady, who had various tattoos on her arms and neck. He told her he liked her tattoos, and asked her where she had them done. She replied and told him that it was literally two-minutes away, from the pub.

As she pulled him a pint of lager, he asked her whether the tattoo parlour did snake designs; she looked at him, as she took the money for his drink and asked whether he was a member of the "Ambleside Sect"? 'I have a friend who belongs to the sect, said Sinan, and will be joining soon, once I have the tattoo done!'

In between serving other customers, the barmaid had given him the location of a large house, in Ambleside Avenue, close to Gleneagle Road, so Sinan thanked her for the information, and said he couldn't wait to get his new tattoo.

He walked back to Gleneagle Road and turned into Ambleside Avenue, where he found the large house, but he couldn't see or hear any noise; it looked empty.

A lady and a man came through the front door of the

house; Sinan glanced at them and walked further on. Sinan then realised that he had seen the man before, and was sure the man was one of their clients at the tattoo parlour, but he continued walking.

The couple jumped into a taxi, which took them past Sinan, so he turned round and walked back to the house and saw several more people coming out. He crossed the road and walked back towards the station, on the high road, then, just as he turned left into Gleneagle Road, someone called out to him. 'Sinan, is that you?

Sinan turned round and saw Iago, who asked him what he was doing in here. Sinan told him he was looking for another tattoo parlour in Ambleside Avenue, and pointed to the shop, with the "For Rental" sign outside. 'So, Rod wants to expand the business, said Iago, that would be handy for me, being so close to where I am staying!'

Sinan breathed a sigh of relief, when he remembered spotting the sign above the empty shop. 'Sinan, said Iago, come with me, I want to show you, my club!'

He led Sinan back to the large house, and opened the front door; they went downstairs into a large dimly lit room, Iago switched on the lights; Sinan couldn't believe the size of the room, it was full of chairs, and there were red velvet curtains at the rear, which looked like they were in front of a stage.

'This is where we have our monthly meetings, said Iago; we have one coming up soon, so you must join us.'

Sinan couldn't see anything that related to snake-worship, but said he would like to attend the next meeting, if it was ok.

Sinan rang Rod and told him about the large house in Streatham, but couldn't see anything that would link it to snake-worship, and also mentioned the empty shop, in the same road, which he used as an excuse for being in the area, so they agreed to speak further, at work the following day.

Iago walked into the shop, and expressed his interest in the shop in Ambleside Avenue to Rod. Rod said that he wanted to expand the business, and had asked Sinan to have a look, next time he was in the area. Iago didn't look convinced, but also mentioned that he had invited Sinan to the next meeting, at his club. 'Sounds good, thank you Iago, said Rod; let's talk about it later.'

Sinan walked in, and asked if anyone fancied a coffee, and produced three cappuccino's, which he made, from the machine recently purchased by Rod.

The day was very busy and seemed to be going very slowly. Sinan had finished with his last client for the day, when a young girl walked into the shop. Iago said he was sorry, but the shop was about to close.

'Gentlemen, said Rod, let me introduce you to my good friend, Maria-Jose!'

'Good to meet you, said Sinan, we have heard so much about you from Rod! '

'Hola, buenas tardes, said Iago, who then kissed her hand, and gave her a wink!

Rod said he would see them tomorrow, and left the shop, holding Maria-Jose's hand.

Sinan looked at Iago and asked him when he would be able to visit one of his meetings. 'Maybe you and Rod can join us next weekend, said Iago; it will be good to see you!'

The following Saturday afternoon, Rod met Sinan at the Bull pub, in Streatham High Road; the barmaid asked them for their order and recognised Sinan. 'Are you meeting up with Maria-Jose this weekend, asked Sinan?'

Rod explained that she was busy over this weekend, and would try and see her during the week, as she was about to return to Spain.

They walked from the pub, then into Gleneagle Road, then turned right into Ambleside Avenue. Rod commented on the size of the houses, and Sinan pointed over to the large house across the road.

They were met at the door by a young girl, wearing what looked like a waitress uniform, and they followed her downstairs, and into the large, brightly-lit hall, with around twenty males and females, standing, drinking and chatting to each other. Sinan looked across at the red velvet curtains, which were closed, and heard movement coming from behind them.

Iago gave them both a beer and introduced them to some of his members, then said he would see them shortly, as he had to arrange a few things. They both saw that some of the people had the "Sugaar" tattoos, on their arms.

Four large men entered the room and asked the guests to move to the back of the hall, then started to lay out the chairs, which had been stacked up, at the side of the curtained stage area.

'Please be seated,' was announced from a voice, behind the curtains!

Once everyone was seated, a man dressed in a black-hooded robe, appeared from behind the red velvet curtains, and started to speak.

'Ladies and gentlemen, welcome to our monthly gathering, for the "Adorador de Serpientes", or for the

benefit of our two new guests, the worship of serpents!'
Rod looked at Sinan, they both knew it was Iago.

The curtains started to open and revealed eight figures, all dressed in the black-hooded robes. The hoods hid their faces, so you couldn't make out, whether they were male or female.

The lights above them started to dim, and a number of coloured spotlights lit up an area, at the back of the stage, where a black velvet drape, covered an oblong shape. Iago gestured to one of the hooded figures, who removed the drape.

It was a large glass terrarium, which had a few small boulders, some tree branches and several snakes inside. Iago removed one of the snakes and confirmed that it was an Australian Black Tiger Snake, which he draped over his shoulders, but clasped its head, and announced that the snake was highly venomous. He then placed it back into the terrarium, and asked one of his assistants to bring forward another snake.

The hooded person produced a basket, with a lid, and when the lid was removed a "Pungi" was blown, which made the snake appear. The snake appeared to be hypnotised; and the audience started to wail and also looked to be hypnotised. One of the hooded figures glared straight at Rod, who could sense that something was not right.

Above the audience, four covered objects began to lower slowly to the floor, in front of the stage. When they landed, the audience could see more snakes, of different species, contained within glass cabinets.

Iago clapped his hands, and four of the hooded figures each stood behind one of the cages., then each lifted out a snake, including a blue Malayan Coral snake, a Russell's Viper, a mainland Tiger-snake, and a Black Mamba. All these snakes were classed as the most venomous, in the world.

Rod and Sinan wondered where this was going, they saw each of the snakes being lifted from their glass cage, with its black-hooded handler being careful and holding the snake's heads.

The audience still looked as though they were hypnotised, then the remaining hooded figures came down the stairs of the stage and walked amongst them.

Chanting started; softly at first, then it became louder. A whirring noise started above the throng, and a large glass cage started to descend from the ceiling, then stopped six-feet above the crowd.

Two of the large men, who organised the seating, stood in front of Rod and Sinan, then grabbed their arms. They both started to struggle, but the men were too strong and had vice-like grips.

They were both positioned below the cage, which then started to descend again, this time, covering them. The crowd were still chanting, Rod looked for Iago, to try and get him to release them, but he was not in view.

The eight black-robed figures surrounded the cage and removed their hoods, Iago then came down from the stage and stood beside them.

Sinan recognised most of the figures, as customers of whom had received a "Sugaar" tattoo, somewhere on their bodies. Rod looked directly into Iago's eyes and said *'Why?'*

Ten snakes were placed into the glass cage, including the viper, the black mamba and the cobra; one of the figures looked at Rod; then he realised it was Maria-Jose. He was confused and looked at her, first with a loving look, then with anger.

Sinan quickly tried to stamp on one of the snakes, but it was too quick for him, he felt a sharp pain on one of his legs and screamed out! Rod grabbed one of the snakes by its neck and threw it out of the cage; it landed in the crowd and started to inject its venom into their bodies.

The crowds still chanted; but two of them slumped to the floor, both emitting agonising screams!

Sinan started to grow weaker, he could feel the venom in his bloodstream and passed out.

Rod saw the cobra coming towards him and managed to lift it and throw it into the baying crowd, but it had already sunk its fangs into his hand.

The glass cage started to lift; four large men appeared and carefully removed each of the creatures, with a snake hook. Once they were all removed, Rod was handcuffed and asked to come out and take a seat. He struggled and tried to confront Maria-Jose, but she was on the opposite side of the cage, then Rod saw Sinan wriggling in the cage, which then returned to the floor.

Rod shouted out to Iago, asking him why he had done this. Iago said that Sinan had lied to him, when he saw him in Ambleside Avenue. 'And *you*, he said, are not worthy of being associated with my sister, Maria-Jose!'

Rod tried to see if Maria-Jose had reacted to Iago's comments, but she kept quiet. He rose up from the chair, but was quickly pushed back, by one of the large men.

Three of the black-robed figures appeared and were carrying a very large sack, which they lifted above their heads and opened it up; the crowd cheered and chanted even louder.

Rod looked at what had come from the sack, and saw one of the largest snakes he'd ever seen.

'This, my friend, said Iago, is a Giant green Anaconda and it is capable of devouring a human!'

'No, *NO*, shouted Rod, this has gone far enough; can't you see that he is dying?'

The large snake slithered towards Sinan, who gradually opened his heavy eyelids. He saw the size of the beast, and tried to look for an escape route, but he was too weak, and passed out again.

The giant snake wrapped itself round Sinan and started to squeeze him, but Sinan was already dead, as he made no sounds. The snake then opened its jaws wide and started to clamp them round Sinan's head. It gulped and writhed violently, then Sinan's body, very slowly, started to disappear. Rod bowed his head, wondering if he was to be next. He looked at Sinan's disappearing body, which he could see was now reshaping the Anaconda's body.

Iago stood in front of Rod and told him that he would probably die from his snake bite, so he would be taken somewhere quiet, to die in peace, then Rod's head was hit by a heavy object; making him pass out!

A week later, Rod woke up in a hospital Intensive Care Ward, with a doctor standing by his bed, and saw him waking. 'Where am I,' asked Rod?

The doctor explained that he was found by a girl, who called an ambulance, which bought him here, to the hospital. He also told Rod that he was lucky to be alive, as they had found some snake venom in his body, which should have killed him, but luckily, didn't!

Rod learned that he was in the Intensive care unit, at St Georges Hospital, in Tooting. He was now out of danger, and was told he would be transferred to a normal ward, in a few hours.

Rod Grainger was released from hospital, four days later; he had plenty of time to put a plan together, while he lay in his hospital bed.

After a month, he had grown a full beard, and had a cap ready to wear; as he wanted to be ready, when he decided to check his tattoo shop, in Balham.

The shop, in Balham High Road, was still called "Tattoo You", which Rod could see, as he stood on the other side of the road, then he saw Iago inside, together with Maria-Jose, who sat behind a reception desk. There were two other tattooists working there, but Rod wasn't interested in them!

Rod checked his bank account and luckily, he still had all his money, so he made a few purchases on eBay, and other sites, then had them delivered to a flat, he had recently rented, in Leigham Court Road, Streatham.

After a further week, he had arranged to hire a hall for a month, so that he could prepare it, for a function. All the equipment he had purchased on-line, was now ready to move in.

Rod sent a letter to the "Tattoo You" shop, and had typed it for the attention of Santiago; the letter contained an invitation for him and a maximum of three guests, to join the opening night of a new, "Snake Worship" club, based in Ullathorne Road, close to the Tooting Bec, and Streatham borders.

Three-weeks later, at 7.30pm, Santiago and Maria-Jose, arrived at the address as stated on their invitation. They walked up the driveway of the large house, and were shown into the hallway, by a very large, black-suited man. They were then offered a choice of beer or wine; Santiago had a beer, and Maria-Jose asked for a red wine. They carried their drinks downstairs, and were shown into a room, and, once they had entered, the door was locked behind them!

Santiago banged on the door, but nobody answered. The lights were dim, but suddenly started to get brighter, as a black-robed figure appeared, at the back of the room and spoke through a microphone.

'Thank you for coming, said a voice, I hope you enjoyed your drink, as it will be your last!'

Santiago shouted out and asked the figure to reveal his face. Rod removed the hood and showed his bearded face; at first, neither of his two guests recognised him, then Santiago shouted. '*YOU*, but you were supposed to have died!'

Rod didn't go into detail, but advised them that their drinks contained a drug, which would make them feel dizzy at first, then although they would be awake, they would be unable to move. Rod then asked them to move forward and take a seat.

Santiago and Maria-Jose sat down and faced each other, the drug had kicked in, and they were unable to move, but could see clearly.

Rod pressed a switch; then a large covered, glass cage started to descend from the ceiling, and hovered above both the seats below. The siblings looked at each other and wondered what was going on, but by this time, the drug had dried their throats, so they were unable to speak.

Maria-Jose had tears coming from her eyes; Santiago just stared ahead.

Rod removed the cover from the glass cage; a large tiger was moving around inside, and started to roar. 'For the death of my friend Sinan, said Rod, you will both be mauled, and eaten by the tiger. I would have used snakes, as you did, but I wanted you to be eaten alive; and by the way, he hasn't eaten for two days!'

Rod handcuffed Santiago and pressed another button; a winch appeared, which Rod clipped onto the handcuffs, then Santiago was lifted from his seat and positioned above the cage. The tiger roared loudly, and started to leap towards the dangling body.

Rod pushed Maria-Jose's chair closer to the cage, so that she could see more clearly. More tears were dripping down her face. Rod pressed another button, and Santiago started to descend into the waiting tiger's grasp. The tiger leapt and grabbed one of Santiago's legs and bit hard into it; there were no screams, just the sound of bones snapping! The winch lowered the body further into the cage; the tiger tore at its prey's neck, then started to devour the rest of the body.

'Now Maria-Jose, said Rod, it's time for you to depart this world; you could have helped me, but you didn't!'

Maria-Jose started to move her body; the drug was starting to wear off; she tried to scream, but nothing happened, but Rod waited until she could speak, he wanted to find out why she had watched her brother kill Sinan.

Maria-Jose's voice started to come back; Rod gave her

some water. She explained that her brother had tricked her into joining his cult and said that he would have her killed, if she didn't do as he asked. Also, she told Rod that her brother wanted to take over the Tattoo parlour, so that he could use it solely for his members and future members of his snake worship sect.

'I could not do anything; he is mad and I thought he would kill me,' she screamed. Also, it was me who called the ambulance, and hoped they would be able to save you!'

Rod looked at her and said thank you, for calling the ambulance, and sorry you had to get involved. 'I had to get rid of your brother, as he was responsible for Sinan's death, and now, that has been accomplished!'

Rod gave Maria-Jose another chance, they continued to see each other, and she introduced him to her aunt, in Chelsea. Rod liked her aunt and when she asked her niece about her brother, she told her that he was doing his own thing, and she had not heard from him.

Rod and Maria were married six-months later, in a church. close to her aunts, in Chelsea. They stayed the night at her aunt's place, ready for their trip to Mexico, from Heathrow, the following day, for their honeymoon; a 3-week holiday, in Cancun.

One evening, they went to a Mexican restaurant in the local town, and the waiter came over with the menu's and asked what they would like to drink. As the waiter passed the menu across to Maria-Jose, his shirtsleeve lifted and, on his arm, revealed the "Sugaar", a pair of intertwined snakes and the distinct wording below them, stating: "Adorador de Serpientes"! Maria-Jose, got up from her seat and told him, that they were not hungry!

78

6: LOVE-LOCKS BRIDGE

The young couple walked arm in arm, across the Hohenzollern Bridge, over the river Rhine, in Cologne, Germany. They had earlier visited the main centre of the city, and had browsed the endless streets, full of shops, bars, restaurants and the magnificent, Gothic Cathedral of Saint Peter, in Domkloster, close to the city centre.

They browsed the thousands of padlocks, on "Love-Locks" Bridge, which were adorned with coloured ribbons, or stickers, then signed with the name of the couples, snapped together and the key being thrown into the river Rhine, below them.

The spaces were becoming harder to find, but Alan and his girlfriend Lesley, went off to find a hardware shop, back in the town, so that they could purchase a padlock, to bring back and find a suitable spot, to symbolise their love for each other.

Alan Painter was a Postman and lived with his parents in West Byfleet, close to Woking, in Surrey. He had worked for the Royal Mail, since his 20th Birthday, four years ago and loved the outdoor life. He even wore shorts, in all weathers and became well-liked, by the people, who he delivered post to, on his route. His day-to-day deliveries covered the streets of New Haw, close to his home.

Lesley Gann, worked in an office, based in Guildford, Surrey, as a trainee accountant. She was 23-years old, and also lived with her parents, in Knaphill, also close to Woking.

The couple had met at a friend's Birthday party and immediately liked each other, probably due to Alan's sense of humour and likeable personality.

They had been together for just over a year and were saving hard, to get a deposit together, so that they could get a mortgage on a property, in the Surrey or surrounding area, so that they could still work for their respective employers.

Over dinner one evening, Alan asked Lesley if she fancied a long weekend away, to somewhere in Europe. Lesley got excited and agreed, but wanted to know where to?

Alan had heard about Cologne, In Germany, from one of his fellow postmen, who had been visiting most parts of Germany, for many years.

'Cologne it is then,' said Lesley. Let's get some dates in our diaries and get something booked!'

The Eurowings flight from Heathrow, took them less than an hour, just four-weeks after they had arranged their leave, with both their employers.

They stayed at the City Class Europa Hotel, which was close to the Cathedral of Saint Peter and a few minutes away, from the main railway station, where they had taken the train, for the 11-minute journey, from Cologne Bonn, International airport.

The padlock they had purchased in the town, was not too large, but just right, so that they could sign their names on it and place a love-heart around the signatures. They returned to the Hohenzollern Bridge and searched for a suitable place, to place the padlock.

They managed to find a small gap, between two large padlocks. Alan snapped open the shackle and looped it around the small gap. They kissed each other, held hands and threw the two keys into the river below. They stood there for a few minutes, kissed again and wandered back into town, to look for a "Hop on/Hop off" bus, that would take them on a tour of the city.

They boarded the open-topped bus, which took them to the Historic old town, the City Hall and the Chocolate Museum.

They spotted a sign stating "Rhine River Cruises" and departed the bus, at the next stop. The river cruise was amazing, with wonderful sights on both banks, all the way along their journey.

That evening, they walked back over the bridge, as they wanted to find their padlock. They eventually found it, but someone else had placed a larger padlock over it, which made theirs hard to find.

Lesley was a little upset, but said it was not a problem, as they would both know it was there. Alan wanted to buy another padlock, a larger one this time, so that they could find it more easily.

The following day, they found the hardware shop in Cologne and purchased a new padlock. They wandered over the bridge once more, to search for another gap. They were lucky and found a suitable space, towards the end of the bridge.

They wrote their names on the new lock, together with a love heart, then threw just one key over the side of the bridge, as Alan said they would be able to move it, if they needed to.

They looked for their original padlock, which was close to the town centre side of the bridge, and noticed that the large padlock that had obscured it, was gone.

'Oh well, said Alan, now we have a padlock on both ends of the bridge!'

'Have you seen the telephone number on our padlock,' asked Lesley?

Alan looked at the small writing and jotted the number down, but told Lesley that it was probably a girl or guy looking for business.

They checked a few more padlocks, but none of these had a number on them. Lesley wondered whether it was an apology for placing a larger padlock over theirs, but thought no more about it.

It was their last day in Cologne, so they walked into the town centre and visited the Cathedral of St Peter once more; so that they could light some candles, for their grandparents and a late friend. They placed some Euros into the box and took 5 candles from the container, then laid them side by side, into the tray of sand. They lit each one, and whispered a short prayer to their late grandparents and their friends.

Lesley had looked at some tourist attractions in their hotel lobby earlier, and asked Alan if he fancied going to the Kölner Zoo. 'It's only a mile and a half walk from here, said Lesley, but we can maybe get the tram back later; coffee and a pastry first though?'

The walk took them nearly 30 minutes and the sights

along the way, were amazing. They both commented that it was ages, since they last went to a Zoo, and were quite excited, when they read that there were more than 10,000 animals living there.

They saw the elephant park, the hippo's, the Nile crocodiles and "Rainforest house, which housed the apes, and was designed so that the visitors could observe the primates at close range, without disturbing them.

Lastly, they saw the feeding of the sea-lions and a grand display of rare birds of prey.

They took the tram back to the town centre, and went back to "Love-locks" bridge, to take a last look at both their padlocks.

The larger one was still in place, which they both touched, and Lesley gave Alan a peck on his cheek, then told him that she loved him.

They walked further on, to look for their first padlock, and saw that a larger padlock had obscured it, once again. Alan lifted it and could still see their original padlock in the same place, with the telephone number still showing. Lesley saw that the larger padlock also had the same telephone number written on it. 'This is weird, said Alan, it's as if someone wants us to contact them?'

'Call the number, said Lesley. Let's find out what this is all about?' Alan tapped the number into his phone, but it wouldn't connect him, so he checked and put in the German area code before the number and let it ring. 'Guten Abend, das ist Steffen!'

'Do you speak English,' asked Alan?

'I do speak English, who is this please?'

Alan explained about the padlock, on the "Love Locks" bridge; there was a brief pause, then the man apologised. 'My name is Steffen, and I am sorry about your padlock being covered, but I cannot explain this on the phone; are you still in Cologne?'

After confirming that it was their last day in Cologne, Steffen asked if he could meet them briefly, to explain the situation, they agreed and met at their hotel bar, an hour later.

'Can I buy you both a drink,' asked Steffen?

Lesley asked for a Gin and Tonic and Alan had a Kölsch.

'I apologise for asking you both to meet me, said Steffen, but what I need to say, I couldn't tell you on the phone.'

Steffen explained that he and his late girlfriend, Maria, had visited the bridge, during a visit, 2-years ago and that they too, had placed a padlock on the bridge. He said that they had also placed a smaller padlock on the bridge and that a larger padlock had appeared the following day, which had obscured the smaller one.

Alan and Lesley wondered why this was happening, but let Steffen continue.

'Maria was quite upset, explained Steffen, and we too, went and purchased another padlock, but a larger one, just as you did; we also found another small place on the bridge, and fitted our new lock, so everything that has happened to you, is exactly what happened to us!'

'Did you say your *late* girlfriend, asked Lesley, what happened, if you don't mind me asking?'

'Maria and I, were engaged, just over 2-years ago, said Steffen, we often came to Cologne, as we have friends here. Eventually, we moved here and rented an apartment, close to the town centre, and we both worked in a bar, just 5-minutes away, from there.'

Alan and Lesley could see the sadness in his eyes, when he told the story, and listened intently.

'We saw the rows of padlocks on the Hohenzollern Bridge, and wanted to place ours there!'

'Did you see a telephone number on your first one,' asked Alan?

Steffen said that they did see a number on their first one, and Maria wanted to make contact. Steffen bowed his head and asked if they would give him a few minutes to compose himself.

Lesley said he should stop telling the story, if it was causing him grief, but he responded by saying it was very important that they listen to the rest of it, then Steffen continued.

'I contacted the number and confirmed that we had found it on the padlock; the man said it was important that they should meet up, as there was something evil about the padlock. He said that he was a government officer, and that people had been placing more than one padlock on the bridge, and also, that some of these people had disappeared and were found dead, a few days later!'

Alan looked at Lesley and they both had the look of fear on their faces, as Steffen continued.

'It was Maria's day off, and I arranged to meet her and the officer, outside the Cathedral, after my shift, but one of the guys didn't turn up for work, so I had to work an extra 2-hours. I called Maria, but she didn't answer, so I left her a text, but she never responded.'

'When I finished work, continued Steffen, I went to the Cathedral, but it was later than we planned, so I called her again, but she didn't answer. When I got home, she wasn't there, and I wondered if she had gone to the bridge. I walked over to the "Love-Locks" bridge and couldn't see her. I then checked our original padlock, and the larger one, that had the number on it, was gone.'

Alan ordered some more drinks and Lesley put her hand on Steffens shoulder, and asked if he was ok to continue.

'I kept calling and texting Maria's mobile, but still had no response. I went to the police and gave them the story, and they said they would investigate the matter. I heard nothing for days and I kept going back to the bridge, to see if she would turn up, but still ….!'

Lesley gave him a cuddle and said he must stop telling the story, as it was making him upset, but he responded by saying that it was very important that they should hear everything.

'I had a call from the police, asking me to join them at the mortuary, as they needed a body identified. I went, as asked, but all the time, I hoped that it wouldn't be *my* Maria! They removed the sheet from her face, and although it looked like her, it wasn't Maria. One of the police officers gave me some coffee, when we had finished the identification, and asked me to meet him at "Love- Locks" bridge, that evening. I met him there, and he asked me to show him the padlocks. They were both still there, so was the telephone number, on the original one. The officer stated that the police were working on a number of cases, involving missing girls and, that all of these cases, were related to the padlocks.' Steffen sipped his drink slowly, then continued.

'I asked him for more information, but he said he was unable to give me anything else, as it was an ongoing case. He also asked if I still had the number that was on the padlock. I gave it to him and he said he would follow it up! The following day, the officer called me and said he had a lead, and would I be happy to answer a few more questions. I agreed, and met him at an address in Cologne, but asked to come alone, and not tell anyone else, as it was a highly confidential case. I thought it was weird at first, but wanted to find my Maria. When I got to the address, he had given me, it was a large house, just outside the town and I parked in the driveway. The officer invited me in and asked if I wanted a drink. I had a beer and followed him downstairs, to a basement area, but I started to feel quite sick, and knew he had "spiked" my drink. He took me into a room, where I could see four slabs, each with a body under a sheet. There was no movement and I started to pull down the sheets, to reveal the faces; then I saw that one of them was Maria!'

Lesley grabbed his arm and said she was sorry.

'*No*, said Steffen; she was still alive; I could see movement in her face; the officer put the cover back over her face and asked if I was ok. Then I was hit over my head and passed out. When I came too, I was tied to a bed-frame. I looked around and saw sharp objects, syringes and other items, that I could only assume were surgical instruments. I couldn't move and the more I struggled, the tighter my restraints pulled. Sorry, I need to use the toilet, can you please give me a few minutes?'

'We understand Steffen, said Alan!'

Lesley said to Alan, that she felt sorry for Steffen, and wondered how many other people had been abducted.

Steffen returned and continued his story.

'I saw the door open and Maria appeared, she was naked, and looked as though she had been drugged; she had bruises all over her body and her arms were covered in needle marks. She told me she was sorry and confirmed that she met the officer at the Cathedral, as planned, then our colleague Christoph, from the bar arrived and grabbed her mobile. She started to loosen my restraints, then Christoph walked in and stabbed her in the neck. She lay there, with blood gushing from her wound; I thought I was next, but Christoph left the room. I tried to comfort Maria, by talking to her, but she was already dead. I managed to get the arm straps free and released the ropes from my ankles. I looked at Maria, she had no pulse, so I grabbed a scalpel and a syringe, then went quietly out of the room and into a hallway. I could hear voices in an adjoining room and saw, who I now know, was a police officer, talking to Christoph. They were taking photographs of the naked bodies; I was fuming, I ran inside and pushed the syringe into the police officer's neck and pressed the plunger. I saw Christoph coming towards me, and used the scalpel to slash his neck; I checked, and they were both dead.'

'We are so sorry for your loss Steffen, said Alan, and thank you for telling us about what happened; did the police follow up after the death of their officer and Christoph?'

'They probably did, replied Steffen, but I was never contacted or given any details about Maria's disappearance, and can only assume that others in the police force were involved, and got rid of all the evidence?'

'Thank you again Steffen, said Lesley, and sorry you had to go through your whole nightmare, it must have been hard for you!'

'It *was* hard, he replied, but I needed to try and make sure this didn't happen again, and you guys were the only ones who contacted me. I go to the bridge every day and check the padlocks; I know it is a laborious task, but if it saves a life, then it has all been worth it!'

Steffen left the hotel and that was the last time they ever saw him.

Both Lesley and David hardly had any sleep on their last evening, they had packed their cases, and left them in the storage area, behind reception, then they walked across the Hohenzollern Bridge, and checked both their padlocks; the larger one still had their names and the love heart on it.

The original one was obscured by a larger padlock, but when they lifted it, they saw a phone number written on it. Lesley wrote the number down, then they walked back to the hotel, to get their cases, before they left to get the train, back to the airport.

Lesley went over to the Concierge's desk. 'Excuse me, she asked, would it be possible to call this number, and put it on loud speaker please; I just wanted to check if our friend is still at home, before we leave?'

David asked her what she was up to; the phone rang loudly, so the Concierge lowered the volume when someone answered.

'Guten Morgen, hier ist die Kölner Polizeiwache!'

'Sorry, said Lesley, to the Concierge, I must have given you the wrong number; I wrote it down earlier, but must have copied the wrong one down!'

They left the hotel and walked across to the train station. 'What was all that about Lesley, asked David?' 'That was someone at the local Police station in Cologne,' she replied.

'So, it still goes on, said David!'

Lesley sent a text to Steffen, and included the number, stating: "This number came from our original padlock on the bridge, it belongs to someone at the local Police Station; just thought you would like to know. Auf Wiedersehen und viel Glück! X"

'Didn't know you could speak German darling, said David?'

'GCSE A Level, darling,' she replied!

The CCTV Camera zoomed in, on an unsuspecting couple, who had just placed a small padlock onto the bridge ….

7: 16 SECONDS

The old grandfather clock chimed at 9pm, on a very cold winters evening, inside the empty house, in Fulham, South-west London.

The owner had left very early, as he had an important appointment, which meant that he would need to be at an address, to carry out a task; a task that could shock, the whole of Europe!

It was 11.30pm, GMT, when the owner of the property in Fulham, was ready for the 12.59am deadline, in an office block, close to Hammersmith underground station.

In Milan, Northern Italy, a man had arrived at his venue and was ready for the 1.59am deadline.

In Berlin, the capital and largest city in Germany, a man had arrived at his venue and was ready for the 1.59am deadline.

In Valencia, the third largest city in Spain, after Madrid and Barcelona, a man had arrived at his venue and was ready for the 1.59am deadline.

None of these four people knew each other, but they all had the same orders.

Three-months earlier, four men were individually contacted by the same man, on the same day and within two-minute intervals, in London, Milan, Berlin and Valencia. The man used the numbers he had on his mobile phone, to make contact with each of them, but did not have to speak.

A signal had been placed within the mobiles of each of the four men, which triggered off an implant, that had been placed into their heads, just over a year ago. They knew nothing about the implant and once the signal had been set off, they all knew what they had to do.

Each of the chosen men checked their watches; there were ten-minutes to go. They set the timers on a large cylinder, which they had found in each of the venues.

At 12.58am GMT, the timer at the London venue, triggered a red LED light, which silently flashed.

At 1.58am CET, in Milan, Berlin and Valencia, the timers each carried out the same sequence.

At 12.59am and 40 seconds, GMT, and 1.59am and 40 seconds, CET, in Milan, Berlin and Valencia, each of the men pressed another button on the cylinder, then counted four seconds, leaving them 16 seconds, to leave the building, by smashing a window.

Each of the buildings were empty, sixteen seconds later. The cylinders had also gone, with no trace at all. The only clue in the top floor of the building, was a few fragments of glass, which landed on the floor, once the victims had jumped out.

The police in London and the other three venues in Europe, arrived at each of the venues, where it was reported that a body of a man had been found, after allegedly jumping from a great height.

There were no survivors; this was checked by the man that had contacted each of them. The chip's that had been inserted into each of their mobile phones, disintegrated, at the target time of 1am, or 2am, in London and Europe.

'Everything went to plan,' stated the man!

On a large vessel, static and hidden behind the moon, a meeting was taking place. The man who had given the instructions to the four men on Earth, had now resumed his normal shape. His name was Forg!

'The four humans did everything they were asked to do, said Forg; and all of them jumped, as instructed, once they had smashed the office windows, I had prepared, and were dead, once they hit the ground below!'

'This is good news,' said the voice, that was telepathically given, to each of the attending crew of ten!

The police officers in each of the London and European cities, were baffled. All four men were identified, in the cities they lived, but none of them had any reasons to commit suicide.

In London, a police detective was assigned to the case. He read through a file, which named the victim as Charles Edwards, 58 years old, single and with no living relatives. He owned and lived in a 2-bedroomed house, in Finlay Street, Fulham, close to the Fulham Football Club ground. He had taken early retirement from his employment with the Royal Mail, just over 12 months ago. He had a good credit rating, had sufficient money in his bank account and had never broken the law.

Detective Inspector Ronald (Ronnie) Chapman, could

find nothing in the file.

He tidied up the paperwork and placed it into the large grey filing cabinet, in the section marked: "Unsolved Mysteries".

Other police officers in Italy, Germany and Spain, had also checked out the details of each of their victims and had all come up with the same conclusions.

Ronnie Chapman needed to pick up the autopsy from the coroner's office in Fulham, so that he could place this into the file of Charles Edwards – Deceased. He checked all the details in the report, when he got back to his office, and found nothing out of the ordinary.

That evening, Ronnie Chapman had dinner with his wife, Lynda, at their home in Barnes, South-west London. They chatted about their days and other things, then Ronnie mentioned the case of the suicide in Hammersmith. He explained the situation and the fact that there was no reason why he jumped from the building.

'Just a thought, said Lynda, has this happened before, in any other places in the UK?'

'Nice one Lyn, said Ronnie. I will check that out tomorrow. Thanks, I should have thought about that!'

Ronnie arrived at his office, at the police station in Hammersmith. He asked one of his admin girls to check on similar suicide cases involving single men, over the past two-years.

An hour later, the admin girl returned and said she couldn't find anything, but had noticed that Interpol had asked the same question; as there were three similar incidents in Milan, Berlin and Valencia.

Ronnie thanked the girl for her valuable assistance and

sent emails, to each of the European contacts.

He was amazed at the response from each of the officers from the three cities and pieced together the information they had emailed over.

He found the same details, with each of the victims jumping from a high building. All of the victims were single, were also the same age, and had never broken the law; but one thing stuck out – The deaths all occurred, at exactly the same time, even though Europe, were one hour ahead!

The aliens had chosen another four men from Earth. Forg was transported to Earth once more and had returned to London. He had been watching the movements of a man from the Putney area and had placed him into a trance. He then placed a miniature electronic implant, within the man's head. Then he removed the back of the man's mobile phone and placed a minute piece of software inside.

Within two-minute intervals, Forg had arrived in Milan, Berlin and Valencia, and had carried out exactly the same adaptions to the mobile phones and also, the invisible surgery.

Forg contacted his crew and confirmed that everything was ready. Four large cylinders were then transported to each of the four venues, with their coordinates sent to each of the four men.

Ronnie Chapman got a call the following morning, from a detective based in Wandsworth, who covered the Putney area and asked if they could meet for lunch.

They arranged to meet at a tapas restaurant, in Upper

Richmond Road, Putney, around 1pm.

There were only six people in the tapas bar. Ronnie shook the hand of Colin Bickley, an old friend from their training days at the police college, in Hendon, North-West London.

'Heard you were working on a suicide case in Hammersmith, said Colin. Similar situation here in Putney, happened around 1am, this morning!'

They had a couple of San Miguel's and a few dishes of chorizo, prawns and some patatas bravas, then walked down to the 18-storey, Putney Wharf Tower, just 10-minutes away.

They both showed their ID's and used the lift, to access the top floor. The offices were empty and ready for a new business to take over. They ducked under the warning tape and walked over to the smashed window.

'Wow, said Ronnie, must have been a very strong man to break that glass. It was a reinforced glass window and would have taken a very heavy hammer, to break through it!'

'Yeh, said Colin, we thought about that, but couldn't see anything inside here, or where he landed!'

They both checked all around the office, but found nothing. Ronnies phone rang; it was the young admin girl at his office. She confirmed that Interpol had reported exactly the same thing had happened again, in Milan, Berlin and Valencia.

'And here in Putney, replied Ronnie. Can you put the details on my desk and also, send a copy over to Detective Inspector Colin Bickley, at Wandsworth!'

'What's going on mate, asked Colin?'

'Not sure Colin, but this is not the first time; it also

happened in Hammersmith and Europe, recently!'

Back at his office in Hammersmith, Ronnie checked the file from Interpol. Everything was exactly the same as the previous suicides, in the same areas of London and Europe. He checked the coroner's report and the details were also the same, but there were some notes written down on the email front sheet, which had a telephone number.

'Mrs James, Coroner's office,' answered the lady.

'Hi, this is DI Chapman from Hammersmith police station; thanks for your number, how can I help?'

Mrs James explained that she had found a small fragment of an unknown metal, inside the victim's brain and had sent it to an expert Metallurgist and awaited his report.

'I will copy you in, once I get the report back,' said Mrs James.

The alien craft transported four more large cylinders, to London and Europe. Forg had returned to each of the destinations and had chosen the four suitable candidates, in each of the cities, but this time, they were not concerned with just killing off the chosen men, they had something far more sinister in mind!

The chosen men had arrived at the given venues, in London and Europe. They checked their watches; there were ten-minutes to go. They set the timers on the large cylinders, which they had found in each of the venues.

At 12.58am GMT, the timer at the London venue, triggered a red LED light, which silently flashed.

At 1.58am CET, in Milan, Berlin and Valencia, the timers each carried out the same sequence.

At 12.59am and 40 seconds, GMT, and 1.59am and 40 seconds, CET, in Milan, Berlin and Valencia, each of the men pressed another button on the cylinder, then counted four seconds, leaving them 16 seconds, to leave the building, by smashing a window, prepared by Forg.

Each of the buildings were now empty. The cylinders all emitted a sharp, green laser beam, which could be seen, for miles around. The beams were aimed at a space craft, the "Mothership", which was high above the earth, then 4 single beams, deflected to Clapham Common, in Southwest London, Parco Sempione, in Milan, Treptower Park, in Berlin and, El Parque de la Rambleta, in Valencia, Spain.

As each of the laser beams hit the four venues, a large invisible circular dome, shrouded an area of 1km, approximately the size of the O2 arena, in London.

The large spacecraft, which had been hidden behind the Moon, contacted the Mothership, to confirm that the invisible domes were now in place and that they and three other spacecrafts, were on course, to land at all the four venues, in one earth minute.

The "cloaking-devices" were already activated, on the four spacecrafts and hovered over the invisible domes.

A total of eight aliens, two in each craft, entered the domes, at each of the four parks. They found a suitable area to place their weapons, in a remote section, inside the 1km, invisible, curved symmetrical structures.

'Mr Chapman, its Mrs James from the coroner's office, are you ok to talk?'

'No problem, call me Ronnie, he replied!'

Mrs James confirmed that she had the Metallurgists

report and was about to email it across, to both him and DI Bickley. She apologised for the delay, but stated that they needed to get verification from NASA, as the origin of the metal was unknown to him.

'Thank you, Mrs James, said Ronnie, the email has just come through.'

DI Bickley contacted Ronnie, confirming that he had seen the email and saw that NASA were involved. They discussed the report and saw that fragments of the metal had been found amongst some space debris, which had been sucked into one of the Lunar Probe vehicles, during a surface scan, on the moon.

'So, said DI Bickley, we are now looking for aliens, here in London, aliens that can be in four places at once, in Europe and somehow, making people jump out of windows?'

'They didn't teach us about that at Hendon mate, replied Ronnie!'

Inside the domes, at all four places in Europe, four teams of two aliens, had beamed down, to each of the venues, and started putting together their equipment. The humans who were already inside, were oblivious to what was happening, except for a black Labrador, at Clapham Common, who was barking at something.

The Labradors owner called for the dog to be quiet, but the barking persisted. The man walked over to his dog and was about to put its lead on, when he saw a red shaft of light, which hit the dog. All the owner could see, was a small pile of ashes! He searched the area, to see where the shot was fired from, but saw nothing.

A lady who had been jogging past, suddenly stopped.

She had seen the red light, which had "zapped" the dog and contacted the police, to report it.

Two policemen arrived and looked for the jogger, who had called them. They could see some people in the distance, but as they got nearer, they felt a tingle in their bodies, as if they had walked through a screen of wet mist.

The man whose dog was killed, was being comforted by the lady jogger. She told them what she had seen and the dog owner concurred. One of the policemen checked the area, but found no evidence of a weapon or anyone who could have carried this out.

DI Ronnie Chapman received a call from DI Bickley. He told Ronnie that there had been an incident at Clapham Common, involving a dog being killed, by a red shaft of light; and that two officers from Clapham Office, had been despatched to the scene.

'Not sure if this has anything to do with the incident at Hammersmith, said Ronnie, but let's wait for the report and go from there!'

DI Ronnie Chapman made a note and started to read more about the unusual metal, that had been found, inside the brain of the man who jumped from the window, in Hammersmith.

He couldn't understand how a piece of metal, which was found on the moon's surface, became lodged in the brain of Mr Charles Edwards - Deceased. He read the report several times, but saw no evidence of the deceased man, being involved in any lunar activities, and without any living relatives, he was unable to obtain any further information; so, he placed the file back into the cabinet.

A crowd had started to gather inside the dome at

Clapham Common. The two police officers called for back-up and a forensics team.

Some of the crowd started to disperse, when a man shouted out.

'There is something preventing us from leaving here!'

One of the police officers went over to where the man stood and saw him with his two hands trying to push against something, but there was nothing there.

The police officer tried to walk past the man, but something stopped him. He touched all around the area and called out to his fellow officer. The area felt like a hard, plastic sheet. More people from the crowd, had seen the officer and started to panic. A stocky man ran over to the police officer and bounced against the surface, of the dome..

More police arrived at the scene, but the police officer confirmed that they could enter the area, but would not be able to get out!

One of the forensic team, produced a spray can, which would normally be used to mark areas, where a crime had been committed. He sprayed the area in front of the police officer and saw that the whole section looked like a glass screen.

'Contact the military,' shouted the police officer!

DI Chapman received a call from DI Bickley's mobile.

'Ronnie, looks like we have further developments at Clapham Common, said Colin Bickley. Apparently, there are people trapped inside an enclosure, made of glass or plastic. Probably some sort of dome?'

'Ok mate, replied Ronnie, I'll meet you there!'

Ronnie contacted Interpol and gave them the details.

The people trapped inside the dome, were starting to panic; the two police officers tried to calm them down, but nobody wanted to listen.

A young girl walked over to one of the officers, she was crying and started to have a panic attack. Her dog whimpered and tried to get her attention, but she had trouble trying to breathe. Something made the small chihuahua stop in its tracks, then a red shaft of light, hit the dog, causing it to disintegrate!

The aliens contacted their leader and confirmed that they had, just over 150 humans inside the dome. They were ordered to allow another 50 more people inside.

The force field was turned off and some of the spectators managed to walk through the dome, including the forensic team, more policemen, with sniffer dogs, and the two detectives, DI Ronnie Chapman and DI Colin Bickley!

The force field was put back into operation and the aliens confirmed that the number of people, were now in excess of 200.

DI Chapman confirmed to Colin, that he had made contact with Interpol and had received reports that at least 200 people had been trapped inside each of the domes.

'Something quite strange though, said Ronnie, every dog that was inside these domes had been killed, by something?'

Although they were trapped inside the dome, most of the people were using their mobile phones, to contact their loved ones.

The armed forces arrived at Clapham Common.

There were over 100 soldiers, armed, ready for action

and awaiting orders!

DI Chapman asked one of the soldiers to call his commanding officer; a stocky man approached the dome and confirmed his name.

'Colonel Brian Hibberd!'

Ronnie Chapman started to confirm the situation, when they heard loud screams! An elderly woman was holding a leash and stated that her dog was there, a few seconds ago, then it had been killed by something, that looked like a red beam?

The colonel asked DI Chapman whether there were any more dogs inside the dome. Ronnie confirmed that two other dogs had been "zapped" and that he had seen at least seven or eight others, but there could be more.

Ronnie received a call from Interpol. The officer confirmed that twenty-four dogs had been killed, at the El Parque de la Rambleta, in Valencia, Spain, and that the same situation was happening in Milan and Berlin.

DI Bickley had just witnessed three more dogs being killed. He spoke to Ronnie and bought the colonel into the conversation. The colonel mentioned that he had received a report about the unknown piece of metal and asked Ronnie if he had received any further clarification from the metallurgists. Ronnie made another call.

People inside the dome at Clapham, were starting to panic again, as each of the remaining dogs were being killed, by a red laser beam. More people hurried across to the area they had come through, in the dome, but the force field was back in operation.

'DI Chapman, hello Mrs James!'

Mrs James, from the coroner's office, had received a call from NASA, confirming that the same, small metal fragments, had been found inside the brain of two of the other suicide victims, in Germany and Spain. She also confirmed that a doctor Gillen, from NASA, would be contacting him. Ronnie thanked her for updating him.

Ronnie advised the colonel and said he would speak to him again, once he received the call. His mobile rang again.

'Hi, is that Inspector Chapman, this is Dr Alec Gillen from the National Aeronautics and Space Administration, in Washington DC!'

'Thank you, Alec, replied Ronnie, I was expecting your call!'

Dr Gillen gave Ronnie a brief account over the metal fragments and stated that there were similarities to silicon, which may have been deposited by visiting space crafts, on their moon landings. He also explained that the metal would need to be melted at over 2000_0 centigrade, if it were to be used to manufacture anything.

'Maybe a weapon, said Ronnie?'

'Affirmative,' replied Doctor Gillen!

DI Bickley saw that more of the dogs were being zapped, but was still unable to see where the beams were coming from. He crouched over the remains of a dog and thought he saw something between a large tree. He went to investigate and spotted something. He walked away from the tree and returned to the edge of the dome.

'There's definitely something here Ronnie, said DI Bickley. Whatever it is, it's not human!'

Colonel Hibberd was informed about the dogs and the movement near the trees. He left the area to make a call, to his superiors.

High above the earth, the mothership received an

update from each of the European Parks, from their two operatives at each site. The ship's commander gave the orders to proceed!

At Clapham Common, green beams started to fire randomly across to everyone inside the dome. The beams looked as though they were x-raying the people, who were now, all in a frozen state.

Nobody could do anything; the armed soldiers outside the dome were helpless. The colonel gave his orders, asking the troops not to fire any shots!

One by one, people started to disappear. The colonel watched helplessly, as men and women were being taken.

After two-minutes, the remaining people were starting to come out of their frozen state. The colonel watched from outside the dome and noticed that a misty haze started to appear. He placed his hand forward; the dome had gone!

It was confirmed that at least 40 women had been taken. DI Chapman and DI Bickley, were still on earth and wondering why they were not taken.

Ronnie's mobile rang; it was his contact at Interpol. The officer confirmed that there were unconfirmed reports, that 50 or 60 persons were taken from each of the three parks, in Italy, Germany and Spain and that a they were all women.

A crisis meeting was held in the MOD offices in Whitehall, London. Interpol were alerted and asked to attend the meeting, by a computerised screen.

Both DI's Chapman and Bickley attended and were asked to bring all the details they had been given.

They saw Colonel Hibberd amongst the attendees and

gave him a polite nod. The meeting took nearly three-hours and after giving everyone their accounts, DI Chapman was asked to liaise with NASA, to see if they could offer any assistance, as they were now certain, that aliens, from another planet were involved.

In the mothership, high above the earth, over two hundred humans had been placed into a transparent capsule. They were still in a frozen state and were unable to move or communicate.

Each person had been x-rayed once more and the numbers were narrowed down to a final total of 40 women. The remaining people were beamed back to the parks, where they had originally been.

On Clapham Common, two policemen, who had been ordered to stand guard around the area where the dome had been, saw some people appear. They ran across to help them, as most of them were quite dazed. One of the officers contacted DI Chapman, to confirm.

Interpol confirmed that the same had occurred in each of the European venues, but that there were still a few persons missing.

Ronnie Chapman emailed his contact at the MOD and then made a call to Dr Gillen, at NASA.

Alec Gillen had received a call from one of his colleagues, with regard to some activity taking place close to the moon. It had been confirmed that one very large spaceship and four smaller crafts, had been located approximately one mile above the moon's surface.

'That's the only information I can give you for now Ronnie, but be assured, we are working on it!'

Ronnie met Colin Bickley for a beer. They discussed the situation and about the details of some of the people that had been taken, from Clapham Common.

'From the early reports of missing people, said Colin, most of the people were young women.'

'Breeding, said Ronnie?'

The following day, both Ronnie and Colin were called back to a meeting at the MOD, at 4pm.

The meeting started, by asking if anyone had any further information. Ronnie stood up and called out.

'Just a thought, said Ronnie, based on the fact that mostly young women were abducted, from each of the four venues; could it be that they were wanted for breeding?'

The panel of military and parliamentary officials, looked at DI Chapman, each with a puzzled expression on their faces. One of the MP's introduced himself and stated that this *could* be exactly what the aim of the alien's mission, was all about.

Dr Alec Gillen from NASA, joined the meeting via the computer screen. He confirmed that the Silicon samples, could be made into weapons against the aliens and that these were actually being manufactured and also, that a manned spacecraft would be ready to be for launching, within three days, subject to permission by the President of the United States.

Everyone in the meeting room were amazed how quickly the US had managed to arrange the spacecraft and weaponry.

'Now, gentlemen, shouted the MP, we now need to come up with a plan of action!'

Drinks were served after the meeting and Colonel

Hibberd thanked Ronnie for his comments. He also congratulated him over his liaisons with NASA, which has not gone unnoticed, by his bosses.

Colin chinked his glass with Ronnies and said he would either get a medal or promotion for his work, or both!

After a final meeting between the American president, NASA and the chief of Staff for defence, it was agreed with Europe, that they were launching four rockets, of which each carried a special spacecraft, with the intention of rescuing the abducted persons.

Each of the Prime Ministers and presidents of the European countries were notified, to confirm the objectives were to be carried out by the United States, and that the launches would all take place, at 0600 hours, tomorrow morning, from both Cape Kennedy and Canaveral, in Florida.

Dr Gillen from NASA was speaking to one of his colleagues, just ten minutes from lift off.

'Just hope the number of years we've been working on our own cloaking device and transporters, will be worth it, said Dr Alec Gillen!'

'Don't worry, exclaimed his NASA colleague, I just hope the few days *we* had, to get these new weapons ready, will defeat these invaders!'

'Five – Four – Three, Ignition, - Two – ONE, we have Lift-Off!'

All four rockets, from the two space launch pads, lifted off, within seconds, after mission control pushed the buttons. The giant monitors in NASA, showed that all four vessels were on course, for their 60 hour journey.

The first-stage booster rockets split away from the

rockets body and descended back to earth and landed in the ocean.

The second stages became detached and also drifted back to earth.

The final stage, saw the release of four spaceships, each carrying four, specially trained astronauts. These crafts would then become "cloaked" and when ready, would uncloak and transport the astronauts, onto the alien mothership

The main ships continued their journey and landed on the moon's surface, with two additional astronauts in each ship, controlling everything and keeping contact with NASA, on earth.

The first two spaceships uncloaked and three astronauts from these, checked their new weapons and were transported to the interior of the mothership.

The aliens were not ready for them, two shots were fired from one of the astronauts, both hitting an alien, who dropped to the ground. Two remaining aliens looked at the weapons and then at themselves, wondering how these humans had managed to build them.

A man appeared and raised his arms above his head.

'Please don't fire, I am a human like you!'

'Can you take us to where the abducted humans are,' ordered one of the astronauts!

'Follow me,' replied the man!

The man and the two aliens left the control room and walked into an adjoining area, followed by the armed astronauts. They saw 30-40 capsules, each containing a human being, and saw that one of them was breathing.

The remaining two spaceships transported six more

astronauts over to the alien's mothership. They saw the two dead aliens, but not their colleagues from the first two spaceships.

They heard voices from an adjoining room and went to investigate. They also saw the capsules, the man and the other aliens. One of the astronauts contacted the moon-based lead ship, to confirm that they had found at least 40 capsules, containing the abducted people and awaited instructions for their transportation.

The man, standing beside the two aliens, started to bend down, as if he was tying a shoelace. He looked at the astronauts and made sure they didn't notice him. He hid behind one of the capsules and telepathically contacted the mothership.

Four aliens appeared, each carrying a weapon, which they pointed at the astronauts. Shots were fired from either side; three of the aliens fell down, the remaining one carefully placed his weapon on the floor.

The man behind one of the capsules, was being watched by one of the astronauts. The man's shape had started to change and before he was back to his alien shape, the astronaut fired at him, leaving him to join his fellow aliens, on the floor. He was wounded not dead and was asked if he could assist in returning the abducted people back to earth, otherwise, he would be eliminated!

Every one of the 40 women were returned to their homes, in London, Milan, Berlin and Valencia.

The American President received messages from all across the world, thanking him and his country.

DI Ronnie Chapman, was awarded an MBE for his

valuable services for his country and was offered a position with the government, which he thanked them for, but said he would think about it.

DI Colin Bickley, was also awarded the MBE and would become a Detective Chief Inspector, for the Metropolitan Police, at a station to be confirmed.

Forg, the alien, was imprisoned on a space station, but was killed, trying to escape.

A year later, a woman from Milan entered the Maggiore Policlinico Hospital in Milan, following advice from her doctor, to get some tests and a scan. The nurse asked for a doctor to come down to the maternity unit. He saw the scan and the movement inside the lady's womb and immediately contacted a government official.

Each of the remaining 39 women, who were abducted, were asked to attend their nearest maternity hospital, in London, Milan, Berlin and Valencia.

8: THE HOUSE AND THE POOL

Spain has long been a favourite for the British people, whether they go for a short break, or maybe with the intention of becoming an Ex-Pat, and purchase their dream home in the Sun.

Mike Riley and his wife Kate, had visited most parts of the eastern coast of inland Spain, due to the Mediterranean coastline, the history, the weather, and the prospect of living their later years in a hotter climate.

After landing at Alicante Airport in September 2021, they picked up their hire car, and eventually found the AP7 motorway towards Valencia. They had watched many episodes of the TV programme, "A Place in the Sun", and had decided to search for a suitable property close to the sea, and not too far from the Airport.

Twenty-five minutes later, they arrived at Sant Joan d'Alacant, just at the end of the long Sant Joan tunnel, and made a right hand turn to the place they had researched thoroughly. They had already pre-booked a hotel for two nights, which overlooked the Mediterranean Sea, and was within walking distance to a few restaurants and bars.

The next day, after a boozy night in one of the local restaurants, and finishing in the hotel bar, they met an Estate Agent in the hotel lobby and commenced their search, in the Sant Juan area.

After being shown several properties by Paco, the Estate Agent, they both agreed that the favourite property was located close to the town of Sant Joan, mainly due to the cost, and the very large swimming pool, which was a bonus they didn't think they could afford, but it had been empty for just over two years.

They arranged to make a second viewing the following day, and as soon as they entered the grounds, they both knew that this was the one.

A month later, it was a cold October day in their house near Woking, Surrey, but Mike and Kate had successfully purchased their dream house in Spain, and were packed and ready, to return to Sant Joan, once more, to finalise everything and also, to receive some new furniture, that would be delivered to their new abode, the following day.

The drive from Alicante Airport was so easy and they knew that they'd made the right choice of area. Paco met them at the Office of the Notaria in Alicante, who passed over the house keys, once they had signed the relevant paperwork, then wished them good luck.

They wanted to buy a few personal items for their new house, and shopped at Corte Del Ingles, where they bought some new bed linen, and a few other items, ready for the furniture delivery the following day, then made their way to Sant Joan, to stay the night at the same hotel, where they had been the month before.

After checking into their hotel, which overlooked the sea, they decided it was going to be a busy day tomorrow, so they only had a few drinks.

After an early start the next morning, they returned to their new house. 'Start of a new adventure darling', Mike stated, after kissing Kate on her cheek.

The buzzer sounded at the rear gate, which made Mike jump, but he knew their delivery was due, as they spotted a large van, outside their new address, at "Calle Pintor Zurbaran"; and watched, as the two Spanish men, unloaded the new furniture, with Kate directing them, to each of the rooms, where the new items would be placed.

It was seventy degrees around 5pm, so they both decided to cool off in their new swimming pool. After a few minutes, Kate felt cold and climbed out, leaving Mike to continue completing several more lengths. 'Wow, Kate, have you seen the Real Madrid flag at the bottom of the pool, exclaimed an excited Mike?

'I have made our bed and put everything else away, so it must be Beer o-clock' called Kate. 'Rude not too' replied Mike.

They sat on two of the four sun loungers, that had been covered and left inside a room, adjacent to the pool, and probably left by the previous owners, then "chinked" their glasses, calling out "Salud"! 'Must get some photo's', Mike called out.

Mike used the camera on his mobile, to take several photos of the house, the pool and the Real Madrid tiled flag, then sent some of them across to his mates in the UK, knowing they would be jealous, and also itching to be invited over at some stage.

Mike's good friend Rob, sent a response almost immediately. 'I knew Rob would be the first to reply', yelled Mike, then read Rob's WhatsApp message, and quickly looked at his photos. He stared at the rear gate inquisitively. 'What's wrong Mike', asked Kate? 'Look Kate, look at the photo showing the rear gate, it's a young girl looking through'?

Kate put a towel over her shoulders and wandered over to the gate, but couldn't see anyone there, so she went back to the loungers and picked up her own mobile, then took several photos of the same area, and a few more, to send over to her friends. Kate looked horrified, she also saw a young girl in two of her photos, and showed them to Mike.

'What's going on here' asked Kate? 'Not sure darling, someone may have been there and we just couldn't see them, it's been a long day, so let's get showered and ready for dinner, then we can maybe ask some of the locals about what we "*think*" we have seen. (*So now he speaks Spanish, Kate mumbled to herself*)

They walked into Sant Joan village, and browsed as they walked past the shops, and made a note of some of a few possible places to eat, but then they spotted a pub called the "St John's", and both agreed to have an Aperitif before dinner.

Mike looked at the pub interior, and thought he was back in the UK; he asked the barmaid if she spoke English before he ordered, and was amazed to hear a Scottish voice responding. 'I am Heather from Glasgow' she said, and I go to Alicante University, where I'm learning Spanish and other subjects. 'Brilliant' stated Mike.

It was not too busy, so he asked Heather if she knew of the house they had just purchased, in Calle Pintor Zurbaran. Heather confirmed that she didn't know the area too well, but that her colleague Santiago may be able to advise them, as he lived close by.

'Call me Iago', please, how can I help'? Mike explained, and showed Iago some of their photos, revealing the young girl who was looking through the rear gate. Iago looked sad as he saw the young girl. 'Please, let's go and sit somewhere quiet, so that I can explain'.

Iago began to tell the worried couple about something that had occurred two years ago.

'On 24th June every year, we celebrate the birth of Saint John the Baptist, and we call it Saint John's Day, or "Día de Sant Joan". On the eve of this special day, on 23rd June, known as "Nit de Sant Joan", we light bonfires and have fireworks in some of the open spaces, close to the town. Myths and superstition say that Witches, Goblins and Trolls will appear on this night.'

Kate glanced at Mike and shivered, 'can we have another drink please Mike'? Iago called Heather to get some more drinks.

Two years ago, on "Nit de Sant Joan", a divorced Mother came to one of the firework celebrations, which was held close to your home in Calle Pintor Zurbaran. The Mother, Maria, attended the celebration, with her only child, 12-year-old Lucia.'

Heather produced a round of drinks, and Iago said he would cover the cost, then continued with the story.

'The fireworks were being enjoyed by the attending local villagers, and about 10.30 pm, a loud bang was

116

heard, followed by a blinding flash across the dark sky. Most of the people were quite scared, but soon, the sky returned to its dark complexion, then suddenly, a loud piercing scream was witnessed by everyone, Maria then shouted 'Lucia has gone, she was taken away, please help me, please, somebody help me!'

'A call was quickly made to the "Policia Municipal", who were just five minutes away from the venue; they arrived quickly, and asked questions to all the attending villagers, and a female Police lady comforted Maria and assured her that they would find her daughter. Maria was distraught, Lucia was her life, so she wandered around the adjoining streets, calling out and sobbing quietly, but nobody had seen or heard anything; Maria then walked back home, in the hope that Lucia had walked back there, but she wasn't there.'

Kate felt sorry for the mother, and grabbed Mikes hand tightly.

'The next morning, on 24th June, the Policia Municipal were called to Maria's home in Calle Pintor Zurbaran, where the lifeless body of Maria was found in the swimming pool, Maria had drowned herself. Lucia had allegedly been seen on many occasions by some of the locals, but after reporting this to the Police, the area was searched, but she wasn't found.'

Mike comforted Kate and assured her that everything would be alright.

'Why were we not informed about this by the estate agent Paco, why, why', cried Kate?

'Please Kate, we will sort this out, we can do some investigations, and try to get some more information.

They thanked Iago and Heather for their hospitality, and made their way back to the house.

Next morning, after a sleepless night, Kate went down to the kitchen and made some coffee, then glanced over at the rear gate. She googled the dates and location into her mobile, and read the newspaper reports, and after scrolling through, found a story about a medium, who was called to the scene of the bonfire celebrations, the day after Lucia had vanished. 'Mike, come quickly, Mike!'

Mike rushed down the stairs and asked what was going on. 'Check out this', said Kate!

Mike read the story, which confirmed that a medium from nearby El Campello, had checked the disappearance of Lucia, and had held a séance shortly after. The medium, known as Emilia, told the Policia Municipal, that she had contacted the missing girl, and Lucia had confirmed that she was looking for her Mother Maria.

Mike checked the story, then googled the stated name of Emilia Rodriguez, who was listed as a medium, and living in El Campello.

'Come on Kate, let's go and find this medium, lets try and sort this out, once and for all!'

They parked their hired car in El Campello, and Kate rang the number she had written down from the google details. The phone rang. 'Hello, this is Emilia Rodriguez!'

'Hello Emilia, I wonder if you can help us?'

Kate explained the story, and Emilia confirmed that they should meet at her flat, above "Bernie's" Bar, which overlooked the sea. 'I will wait for you outside the bar', Emilia confirmed.

An hour later, Mike and Kate took Emilia back to their new house. Emelia sensed that Lucia had been there, and suggested that they carry out a séance, so that she could speak to Lucia.

An inquisitive Kate asked Emelia why this was not carried out when she had spoken to Lucia, two years ago. 'Because nobody believed me', replied Emelia!

A Table was carried over to the swimming pool, and three chairs were placed around it. Emelia called out. 'Now, we must all hold hands and *please*, do not let go, that is very important!'

'*I call upon Lucia Fernandez, Lucia, please confirm if you are here?*'

They heard nothing, but then, Kate went very cold! 'Keep your hands tight please, I can feel a presence', exclaimed Emelia.

'*Is that you Lucia, please speak to me*', Emelia called out several times.

Kate's eyes closed then opened wide, her eyes rolled and she spoke in a strange voice.

'*I am Lucia, I am looking for my mother, my mother Maria Fernandez, please let me know where she is, please, please help me*'!

Kate's head slumped forward. Emilia called out; '***Keep your hands together, please, do not let go, we are close to getting contact!***'

Emelia confirmed to Lucia, that they had spoken before, and that she, together with the couple, were there to help.

Kate spoke once more, with the voice of Lucia.

'All I want is to find my mother, can you help me?'
Emelia confirmed that they would help her find her mother, but needed to ask some questions, so that they could piece together the night she disappeared. Kate spoke again.

'There was a loud bang and a very bright light in the sky, said Lucia, I was then grabbed by someone dressed as a witch that night; the witch put her hand over my mouth, and I couldn't scream out. I was taken to a place outside the village, and cannot remember much after that, except that I was physically hurt by this person and soon after, everything went dark.'

Emelia spoke and stated *'Lucia, soon after your disappearance, your mother unfortunately took her own life, I am so sorry, but she could not bear the thought of you not being with you.'*

'I understand thank you, (sobbing was heard) is there a way that I can be with her again'? Kate was becoming frightened, but carried on.

'There is a way Lucia, said Emelia, but we need to make sure you understand what to do. You must come to your old house, and enter the swimming pool, this is where your mother died, so you must enter the pool, and then, you will be together once more!'

'I do understand, said Lucia, I am standing outside the gate now, and will do as you ask'.

'Please remain seated and hands together, asked Emelia.

A blurry figure of a young girl appeared at the side of the pool and walked down the steps. *'Mother, now we will be together again once more.'*

Mike, Kate and Emelia told their story to the Policia Municipal, shortly after the events, and after an investigation of the events that occurred two-years earlier, the police arrested a woman for the abduction and murder of Lucia Fernandez.

Kate and Mike went for a celebratory drink at the St John's Pub, that evening and touched the plaque outside, and both stated, 'Thank you, Saint John!'

9: ALLIGATOR ALLEY, FLA

Florida, USA, attracts many people from all over the world, looking for sunshine, good food and adventure.

Many of the resorts, from the "Panhandle", down to Miami and the Florida Keys, have been the holiday destinations for couples, friends and families, depending on whether you want to see the attractions of Disneyworld, Busch Gardens, Universal Studios, or the white-sandy beaches, and the endless coastlines.

Greg and Mandy Wilson had been saving for their "dream Holiday", for over four years; They chose Florida, "The Sunshine State".

Greg Wilson was a delivery driver, working seven days a week, but he enjoyed working outside, rather than sitting in a stuffy office.

Mandy was a beautician and worked at her sister's hairdressing salon, four days a week.

The couple, once they had married in 2005, agreed that they did not want children and their life revolved around their vacations, once they had saved enough money.

For the last four years, Greg and Mandy worked very hard. They travelled to Brighton, Southend and other coastal resorts every year, just for a few days, here and there, during their 3-week annual holidays.

Their local travel agency had found them some reasonably priced return flights to the states. They would fly from London Heathrow, to Tampa. A hire car was included as part of the package, which they would drive for just over an hour, to the resort of Captiva

They had pre-booked a five-day stay in a luxury apartment, on Captiva Island, which was local to restaurants and of course, the magnificent beaches.

After their five-day stay, they would drive down to Miami and the Keys, stopping at various resorts on their way, hoping that vacancies were available.

'Only one week to go Mandy,' called Greg, as he poured a fresh cup of tea, after their early breakfast. 'I can't wait darling, replied Mandy. it's been four years since our last long-haul trip and next week, we will be on our journey of a lifetime.'

Greg kissed Mandy on her cheek and left for work. 'Bye darling, see you later,' he called.

One week later, on 4th June, 2016, Greg and Mandy Wilson arrived for an early flight from
Heathrow Airport, to Tampa Florida. The flight would take about 12 hours, a lot longer than their usual European journeys of 2-4 hours.

They landed at Tampa Airport on time, and after clearing immigration, walked across to the Car Hire desk.

They were on their way to their destination after driving over an hour, and searched for a restaurant to stop and eat. They found a Denny's Diner in Sarasota. It was nearly 2pm in the afternoon, already, their body clocks were "out of synch", with the six-hour, earlier time difference.

They continued their journey after lunch and after passing through Fort Myers, saw the signpost to Sanibel and Captiva Islands.

They made their way to Jensen's on the Gulf, which was situated at the very end of the main road, once they had crossed the bridge, past Sanibel Island.

They were made very welcome by the lady receptionist. A porter was called, who carried their luggage and showed them to their luxurious apartment, overlooking the Gulf of Mexico.

Later that evening, they found a restaurant within walking distance. The name made Greg chuckle. 'R C Otters,' said Mandy, who also laughed, once she made the connection.

They ate the seafood and drank beer and wine, with music supplied from a local guitarist, playing Jimmy Buffett tunes. 'This is paradise, Mandy said, as she planted a red-lipped "smacker", on Greg's lips.

They wandered towards the beach, to check out the area and found a pub called the "Mucky Duck". 'Nightcap darling,' called Greg?

They thoroughly enjoyed their brief stay on Captiva Island and packed their bags into the boot, ready for the next part of their journey, towards the Florida Keys.

They drove along "Alligator Alley" and after a couple of hours, saw the signs to Miami and the Keys.

They decided to stop for lunch in Miami and managed to park close to a Columbian Restaurant, overlooking the beach.

After lunch, a guy with a Spanish-sounding accent welcomed them to Florida and asked where they were heading. 'We're travelling down to the Keys' said Greg, but said no more, following the glare from Mandy.

The guy gave them a card and asked them to check out a Haitian Restaurant in Key West, if they were going there. He walked away from the couple, and tipped the brim of his Panama Hat.

Mandy told Greg she did not like the man, but Greg said he was only being friendly.

They arrived at a Motel in Key Largo, and spotted a "Vacancies" sign outside a medium sized Motel, which overlooked the bay.

The next few days were spent, checking out and stopping overnight, at other resorts, including Islamorada, Marathon, Big Pine Key and finally, Key West.

It was quite busy in Key West, but they checked into a Motel, close to the main town.

That evening, the happy couple wandered around the town centre and stopped in a bar.

The music was a mixture of Caribbean and other styles, but after a couple of Margarita's, they quite enjoyed the easy-going rhythms.

Most of the restaurants were packed, people were queuing outside, waiting for tables. Greg checked his pocket and pulled out the card, the guy had given to them in Miami.

'Look Mandy, said Greg, that restaurant over there is the one that guy recommended to us; come on, let's give it a try, it's busy but there are no queues!'

They got a table straight away, thanks to another couple being finished and having paid the check.

They ordered some drinks, when the waiter arrived with the menus. He had confirmed that the fish was fresh and had been caught earlier, so a selection of mixed fish was ordered, together with a bottle of Californian white wine.

They enjoyed their dinner and commented on the friendly ambience; then a young girl appeared on the small stage.

The girl started singing in an unusual but soothing manner, which made all the diners look up and across to her. The song they assumed, was from Cuba, but it was Haitian.

Generous applause was offered by everyone and an encore was called for, once she had taken her bow.

Greg and Mandy had thoroughly enjoyed their evening and most of the diners were starting to vacate the restaurant. The waiter issued the check and asked if they would like a drink on the house. 'Rude not too,' said Greg.

They wandered back to their Motel, which was not too far away. Mandy said she felt quite dizzy and Greg confirmed that he too felt slightly "squiffy". Mandy laughed at Greg's words and passed out. Greg's eyes were getting heavy and he too, passed out.

Greg and Mandy woke up, but not in their Motel, they had no idea where they were, or how they had arrived at the room, where they had slept the night.

'Where the hell are we' asked Greg.

Mandy couldn't give an answer.

Mandy wandered over to the door. The door was locked! Greg looked out of the window and all he could see was a dirty old road and the odd, old tatty vehicle, passing through.

Greg banged on the door several times and shouted, asking for someone to let them out. They heard the sound of a key being entered into the door lock.

A man stood before them and asked them to follow him. They both questioned him about where they were, but he did not respond.

Greg and Mandy followed the man downstairs and were asked to sit quietly, on a moth-eaten sofa, which was quite smelly. Mandy said she would prefer to stand.

'Sit, shouted the man. They both sat down and started to ask questions, but still there was no response. Then the man spoke.

'You are still in Florida' he said, but not in the Keys. Both of them looked at each other and wondered how they had got there.

A young girl came in through the front door and greeted the shocked couple. It was the singer from the restaurant.

They fired the same questions to the girl, but she too would not respond. The man whispered to the girl and she went into the kitchen.

Greg and Mandy were afraid, they whispered to each other, stating that they had been kidnapped, but without any response from anyone, wondered why and what they were doing in this strange place.

The young girl returned from the kitchen and bought a plate of fried chicken, walnuts and rice, together with two glasses of water. The girl advised them to eat and drink now, as they may not get anything else that day.

Greg asked the girl what the dish was, in a soft voice, trying to be friendly and get some answers. Still, she did not reply.

Mandy stood up and screamed. '*Who* the hell do you think you are, why are we here, what do you want from us!'

The man asked them to eat and drink something and would explain afterwards.

They both ate some of the meat, but their appetites were all over the place, due to their uncertain predicament.

Shortly after, the couple were asked to follow the man outside, to the back of the property.

They looked around and saw several rusty old vehicles, which looked as though they had been completely stripped of any spare parts.

The man and the girl confirmed that they had been taken from the Keys and were now in a place called Felda, in Hendry County, which is close to Alligator Alley, on the Tamiami Trail.

'But why are we here, asked Mandy and what do you want from us!'

'You have been chosen to participate in a ceremony, stated the man. Tonight, you will join us for a celebration of some magical rites, something that our people still practice and enjoy, every year. That is all I can say for now.'

Greg and Mandy were shocked, 'Magical Rites' Greg muttered. Mandy started to sob and screamed *'Why us!'*

They did not get a response from either of their captors and again, started to feel quite dizzy. 'I think we've been drugged again said Mandy, as her eyes closed.

The owner of the motel in Key West, had been banging loudly on the door, but after 5 minutes, used his pass key to access the room. He saw that the couple had left some empty bottles and clothing in the room, but their suitcases were gone.

He contacted the Monroe County Police and reported that the couple from England had vacated the room, after one night, but had paid for three nights. He also confirmed that the credit card they had used to pay, was showing no funds, when he had contacted his bank. Monroe Police stated that they would send an officer over.

Greg and Mandy woke up, but still felt drowsy. They were now in a different place and they could hear bongos being played, very loudly. They could also hear chanting and wailing. Greg looked out of the dusty window and shouted, *'NO WAY*!'

Mandy looked at him and asked what he had seen.

'There are men and women with painted faces and wearing bird-feathers on their bodies, said Greg. They are also wearing teeth around their necks; but also, I can see a pool with Alligators!'

Mandy started crying and couldn't understand why they were at this place and what was going to happen to them.

The police officer arrived at the motel and took the pass key from the owner. He entered the room. and searched it thoroughly, but all he could find, was a business card for a Haitian restaurant in Key West. He returned to the police station and reported to his sergeant. 'Looks like we may have another abduction sir, stated the police officer, only this time, we could have a lead!'

He passed the business card to his sergeant.

Two police officers entered the Haitian restaurant in Key West and asked to speak to the owner; the young girl confirmed that he was out on business and would possibly be back in time for the evening service.

'Can you answer a couple of questions please, asked one of the officers?'

After questioning the girl for a few minutes, she broke down in tears and told the police officers that she had nothing to do with the kidnapping and that she would have been killed, if she did not do as she was told. 'Where are they now, asked one of the officers?'

One of the officers returned to his vehicle and contacted his sergeant. 'Sir, he said, the English couple have been taken to Felda, in Hendry County and it looks like they will be killed this evening, at a Voodoo ritual!'

The sergeant rang the Sheriff's office in Hendry County and gave them the details.

Greg and Mandy Wilson watched from their room and looked at the commotion outside. The men and women were dancing and looked as thought they had been drugged. One of the men, who they assumed was the leader, held a goat by its body, then produced a large knife. The crowd were chanting and some appeared to be having convulsions. The man then slit the throat of the animal and drained the blood into a container, which was shaped like a goat's skull.

The crowd cheered and ran towards him, hoping that they would be fed the blood from the skull.

Greg looked around their room, hoping to find something to use as a weapon, but there was nothing. Mandy sobbed loudly and cuddled into Greg. The chanting and wailing became louder!

The couple were taken from their temporary prison and marched out to face the baying crowd. The leader then produced some secateurs, he grabbed Greg's arm, and gripped his wrist very tightly; he then cut off the little finger of Greg's left hand and threw it over to the pool. A large Alligator appeared and swallowed the digit!

Another man appeared and was holding some rope. Greg recognised him; it was the man that gave him the business card, in Miami. '*WHY*, why are you doing this to us,' shouted Mandy. She then comforted Greg, who was in pain, and told him that she loved him.

Both the captives were bound by their wrists, with the rope, then their ankles were tied. Two stocky men appeared, and carried each of them over to a large tree by the pool. A rope was thrown over one of the branches; then they looked over to the couple, who were both quivering and unable to retaliate.

'Who will be first,' asked one of the stocky men. 'I will go first stated Greg, but please let my wife go, please I beg you!'

Greg was positioned below the tree and the dangling rope was passed through his bound wrists. The man

131

pulled the rope tight and faced Greg. 'Mask or no Mask,' he asked!

'Just get on with it, you ....' The man pulled the rope and raised Greg, he then produced a long stick and prodded the struggling body. The Alligators were watching and waiting, looking up at the swinging body of their next meal;

Greg called out to Mandy and for some reason, apologised.

Blue and red flashing lights appeared, together with loud sirens wailing; an officer with a bullhorn, gave a short, sharp message to the wailing throng. '*LOWER THE BODY, VERY CAREFULLY*'!

The stocky man did as he was told and gently lowered Greg's shaking body to the ground. Mandy had managed to loosen her rope shackle from her wrists, then untied the ankle restraints.

She ran across to Greg and gave him an affectionate embrace, then saw the Haitian man coming towards her. He pushed Greg to one side and grabbed Mandy, and shouted at the officers, stating that he would throw her to the Alligators, if they did not leave.

Greg painfully removed the rope from his ankles and stealthily crept over to the Haitian man, he then gave the man a sharp blow to his neck, which made him release Mandy. Greg then gave the man a heavy punch, which stunned him. Mandy backed away from the melee, and ran over to one of the police officers.

The Haitian man was in pain and started to throw punches at his attacker, but Greg was too quick and angry, to receive any more pain. They both fell to the ground and the man had his back to the pool.

A very large Alligator appeared, and snapped his jaws around the Haitian man, then returned to the pool with him. The Alligator rolled its body in a circular motion, with its jaws wrapped around the Haitian man's body, then disappeared, leaving a large number of bubbles, and pools of blood, above the surface.

The police officers rounded up the crowd, and a paramedic put a temporary dressing over the remains of Greg's missing finger. Greg and Mandy were taken to the Hendry regional Medical Centre, where they were both checked over, after which Greg had received a dozen stitches.

A few days later, the couple attended the Sheriff's office in Hendry County, to give their account of the ordeal; the Sheriff thanked them for helping them to catch the perpetrators.

'We have made arrangements for your return home folks, confirmed the Sheriff, and we have laid on a "stretch Limo, to take you to Tampa Airport, tomorrow afternoon.' He then passed Greg an envelope with their flight tickets, and thanked them again.

At the airport, Greg opened the envelope to produce the tickets and spotted another envelope inside, when he removed them. He passed it to Mandy who read out the words. "Do not open this until you are on the plane home"!

Greg and Mandy flew back in British Airways "Club-Class" and were given a glass of champagne, by the Air Stewardess. Mandy produced the envelope and opened it; inside was a letter of thanks from the Mayor of Hendry County, stating that they were welcome to visit Florida whenever they wanted, and at no cost to them.

Pinned to the back of the mayor's letter, was a cheque for twenty-thousand US Dollars. 'That will cover the money they stole from our credit card,' said Greg. Greg chinked Mandy's glass and said 'Cheers!'

The leaders of the illegal "Voodoo" ring, were all imprisoned and sentenced to life, with no parole. Others, who were found to be part of the abominable crime, were imprisoned for sentences ranging from eight to fifteen years. 'Just a thought, said Mandy. If these people were sent for trial, for the crimes they committed, why were we not summoned to give evidence?' 'I can only assume they have a different system to ours, in the UK,' replied Greg? Mandy thought about it, and said there were still a few discrepancies, and asked another question.   'Did you notice the Sheriffs tattoo, when he shook your hand Greg, she asked; because I saw a similar one on the man who cut off your little finger?' Greg responded with, 'I was a bit busy when he snipped my finger off,' he replied.

The tired couple arrived back at Heathrow, on time and were just glad, that their unpleasant experience was now over.

Mandy "googled" the newspapers for Hendry County, and found the "Clewiston News", where she saw a photograph of the Hendry County Mayor, shaking the hand of the local Sheriff. She called Greg, and asked him to look at both their hands, as they both had the same tattoos.

A young couple on honeymoon, were visiting Miami and were passed a Haitian restaurant's business card by a Spanish speaking man. They thanked him, then tore the card up and threw it in the nearest waste bin!

10: THE VISITORS

It was quite misty across Horsell Common that morning; it was just past 6 am, and the sun was about to emerge from behind some cotton-wool clouds. There was nobody to be seen, albeit, the foggy outlook would have hidden anyone, who happened to be there.

The mist started to disappear, and a mysterious man appeared from behind the thick trees; he was checking around the sandpit area, with great interest. He held a circular object, which emitted barely audible bleeps, similar to a metal detector, but without a handle.

He suddenly stopped and leaned over, to check a particular spot, as the bleeping had turned to several lights flashing in sequence, when the apparatus was held above the uncut grass.

He then produced a small cylindrical shaft, about the size of a fountain pen, and waved it just above the grass, then looked around, but spotted no one, so he pressed the end of the shaft, and a blue glow surrounded the grass area.

Approximately 12 minutes later, a vapour trail was hurtling towards earth, just above Horsell common; the speed of the craft was far quicker than any jet-plane or missile, used on earth.

The craft stopped, then hovered over the common, scanning every inch of the 880 acres. Then, whoever was piloting the craft, spotted someone.

The mysterious man looked up and saw a large circular spacecraft, so he switched off the shaft, and placed it into his jacket pocket. He then opened a small rucksack he'd had over his shoulder, he removed the detector, and placed it into the bag.

The spacecraft still hovered above him, but started to make its descent towards the ground. It landed without any sound or lighting, then became invisible. The mysterious man decided to wait, to see who or what would emerge from it.

A transparent orifice appeared at the side of the craft and behind it, there were two figures; they were not human.

The mysterious man watched as the two aliens approached. He had not seen any living thing shaped like this, but he stood firm, until they were in front of him.

Each alien had four arm-like appendages, on their small bodies; two on each side. Their heads were oval-shaped, and the eyes were bright and wide. They didn't have a nose, just two small slits and their bodies were a shade of dark-green, but their four legs and arms were much darker.

Communication with the mysterious man was made by telepathy, in a language he could not understand, but soon, they managed to search their memory banks, and found a language that they both understood.

They discussed their presence at the common, stating that they had heard some strange bleeps. The mysterious man wondered how far the bleeps could have been heard, but accepted the excuse.

The aliens asked why he was searching this particular area on Horsell Common, and answered them, stating that he had lost something valuable, many years ago.

Unbeknown to both parties, they were all being watched. An elderly man was out walking his dog, and was hidden behind some trees, but then the dog barked, "loudly"!

The bark stopped the conversation, and the two aliens disappeared into their craft; the mysterious man waved at the dog walker, then walked over to him, and explained that he was talking to himself, something that he often did, when walking out alone.

The old man stated that the spot where he had seen him, was riddled with alleged sightings of UFO's and strange occurrences, since a book about Martian landings was written, back in 1897, by a man called HG Wells.

The old man then tipped his hat and waved at the mysterious man, and walked away.

Back at the sandpit area, the mysterious man looked around, but couldn't see or hear the aliens, and continued with his search.

The disc's lights began to bleep and glow once more, but this time, they suddenly stopped, just as the cylinder was above a small aperture below. He looked around once more, but he was still alone, so he focussed on the aperture, and his eyes turned red.

His x-ray vision had spotted something, approximately three-feet below the surface; it was a metallic object. He checked once more, after hearing some noises behind him, but could only see a motorbike being driven at high speed, on one of the access roads, adjacent to the common. The mysterious man's body started to contort and writhe; then he'd changed into a small "mole-like" rodent; he was a "Shape-shifter"!

The aliens were still in the vicinity, they were still invisible, but were curious to know just what the creature had found.

The rodent shape-shifter burrowed his way further into the aperture, and saw an object protruding from a wooden crate, which was just what he was looking for.

He removed the object and climbed back to the side of the sandpit area, and returned back to his former "human" shape; the mysterious man was back and he was holding what looked like a weapon.

The aliens reappeared and asked him what he had found. He explained that it was left there many years ago, by one of his colleagues, when they had landed on earth.

He also confirmed that their plan was to eliminate the human race, so that his people could live in peace, and that they had managed to start building colonies on earth, but were struck down by a strange illness, which took the lives of too many of them, so the survivors returned to their home planet. 'This object is a smaller version of a "Heat-Ray", the man stated, but its power is a thousand times stronger than the larger heat-rays our ships were equipped with!'

The two aliens asked to see what it could do, but the man declined, and told them that it would need to be repaired, so he had to get it back to his planet, the home that the earth beings had named as "Mars".

'If you will not give us the weapon, then we will take it from you', replied the alien.

'As you wish, he said, but firstly, can you tell me where you are from?'

The visitors told him that they too, had been to the Horsell Common site many years ago, and had taken the shape of the humans. 'We had lived alongside the earth people, undetected for years and then, the alien confirmed, but we were obliterated by your kind, when you came to attack and based your crafts here, at Horsell Common!'

The man offered an apology, and handed over the weapon, as a goodwill gesture, confirming he did not want to get involved in a further conflict.

The aliens thanked him and returned to their spaceship, taking the weapon with them.

The man watched them board their craft, which then reappeared from its invisible cloak. The silent craft powered up and started a slow descent, then just as the engines were about to go on full-thrust, the mysterious man aimed his circular disk at the spaceship, then sent a small beam direct into the craft. The spaceship vapourised and became just a shower of fine rain, which settled on Horsell Common. 'Maybe that will put an end to their travels to earth,' said the mysterious man. Now I can contact my race, and tell them that the hundred "Miniature" Heat-Rays are now ready, and we can now plan our invasion of the earth once more, and this time, we will have sufficient cures for the diseases the humans carry!'

The "Shapeshifter" changed his appearance to his alien form, and used his cylinder, to contact an awaiting spaceship.

An odd shaped spacecraft arrived, and beamed the mysterious traveller aboard. They would now return to their home; the planet the earth people called "Mars"!

11: INTO THIN AIR:

Colin Parker exited Oxford Circus Station and made his way over to Upper Regent Street, looking out for the BBC building.

He had planned this journey for months, after hearing he had passed the tests, and would be joining the General Post Office, (GPO) as a Messenger Boy, at the Western District Office, in Wimpole Street, London. His A-Z map had told him to turn left into Margaret Street, and then to proceed across Cavendish Square, so all being well, he would be at his new place of work, within five minutes.

Colin suddenly started to shiver in fear, not knowing

what he would be walking into, who he would see there, and whether he would fit in with the other guys.

Colin descended down to the basement of 1a Wimpole Street. below the Main Post Office above, at 0.759 hours, as instructed in his acceptance letter, and walked through the heavy black door, then into the first room on the left. There were at least a dozen or more young lads in the room, all smartly dressed in their GPO uniforms, with blue serge trousers, complete with a narrow red stripe down each outer side of the legs, a lightweight summer jacket, black "Highly Polished" Boots and around their waist, they wore a black pouch and belt. An older man, who was not in uniform, greeted Colin and asked him to go to the office along the corridor, where he would be met by a PHG (Postman Higher Grade) who was on duty that morning. He entered the small room and saw two other boys, who were not wearing a uniform; they too had also started that day. Each of the new employees were given some paperwork to complete, (Official Secrets Act was written on top of the first page) together with an armband, to confirm their identity, until they received their uniforms, which would ready in a week.

Colin Parker was not happy with his secondary school, or the whole the education system, during the early sixties, and after discussing this with his parents, they agreed that he should find employment, which included Further Education, so that he could possibly get some qualifications, to ensure he had a bright future ahead. He really wanted to be a journalist, reporting on anything to do with science and the paranormal, but without any qualifications, he would have to look elsewhere, for now, so after searching through the wanted ads, and also signing up with the local Labour Exchange, he found that the GPO were looking for Fifteen-year-old boys, to become Young Postmen, which also offered a day release at a college, subject to passing some oral and written tests. In September 1965, he had started the first day, of his new career.

The morning went quite quickly, and soon they were taken upstairs, to get some lunch, where they sat together with other messenger boys, Postmen and P&TO's (Postal & Telegraph Officers) Lunch was similar to school dinners, but the atmosphere was totally different, it was a paid job and lunch was free.

After lunch Colin accompanied a senior Messenger boy called Phil Barton, out onto the street above, where he was told just to watch, listen and observe what he would be expected to do, once he was ready to be let loose, once he had been kitted out with his new uniform.

Colin lived in Streatham, South-west London, with his parents and a younger sister, he loved to visit the local swimming pool, where he would meet his friends and a group of girls. He had a crush on one of the girls, named Lyn, who was also fifteen and lived in the same road. Lyn was quite fond of him, but a quick cuddle and kiss was all that was on offer, due to their ages. Colin's sister was a year younger, and they got on well; his father enjoyed watching Fulham Football Club, only if they were playing at home, and his mother worked in a local sweet factory, and often bought home lots of chocolate and other confectionary.

Phil Barton was a friendly chap, he spoke about his love of cars, and told Colin that he couldn't wait to get his driving license, so that he could start driving. They got on well, as they spoke about girls, music and films, everything that they both had in common

They arrived at the London Palladium Stage Door, where Phil passed several greetings Telegrams to the stage door Manager, who sat behind a glass screen. Phil explained to Colin, that they were probably celebrating someone's birthday. and also, that inside the theatre, they were probably rehearsing for the Television Show, "Sunday Night at the London Palladium". As they exited the Stage Door, Bruce Forsyth passed them; Colin looked at Phil, as if to say 'Was that?'

A week later, Colin received his uniform, which he hurriedly put on; and breathed a sigh of relief, when it fitted him perfectly; he was also given a shiny new pouch and belt, which he put on and paraded round the rest room.

Colin was summoned by one of the older boys, and asked to make his way up to the first floor, to receive some instructions about going out on his own; he rushed up the stairs, and was met by four heavyweight messenger boys, who grabbed him and bundled him into the toilet, where they turned him upside down, and lowered his head into a bowl of smelly, black water, with unknown things floating on the surface. There was no point in struggling or fighting, this was his welcoming committee and the ceremonial "Bogging", one of the many initiations that were part of becoming one of the lads, and from that day on, he was one of them, he was now a "Mopper"!

Over the weeks, Colin loved walking round the streets delivering the telegrams and express letters, and quickly managed to learn the shortcuts across the West End, as all the WDO Moppers were on foot. He had also started socialising with some of his colleagues, and even joined the office football team, with their home games being played at Regents Park. The away matches were played on Hackney Marshes and other football pitches, close to the other London postal areas.

Lyn Maberley was a very attractive girl with long blonde hair, and most of Colins friends were envious of him, and when they went to a local dance, she was always the girl everyone wanted to be with, but she always responded with 'I already have a boyfriend!'

Now Colin was earning from his employment, even though it just under £5.00 per week, and after giving his mum thirty shillings, he had enough to take Lyn out to various places, including the Locarno Dance Hall, or one the Cinema's in Streatham. He always made sure that Lyn chose where *she* wanted to go, and what film *she* wanted to see, as this kept their relationship steady, and Colin hoped they would stay together forever, but it was too early to think about their future, after all, they were still only fifteen years old.

It was early October, and the weather was turning cooler, so it was time to wear the winter uniform, which was provided to each of the Messenger Boys, when they started their employment; so, it was time to say goodbye to the lightweight summer jacket, and hello to the heavier blue jacket.

There were not too many telegrams or Express letters for delivery on the Monday morning, so Colin was sent to the Mount Street Branch Office in Mayfair, along with two other Messengers, where they would be asked to pick up a local package or other items, and take them to an address, which would probably be outside the West One area. (Colin had heard many stories of Messenger boys taking parcels to all parts of the UK, even to Europe or further, but as he did not have a passport, *(yet)* he wouldn't be able to travel)

After waiting for over an hour, Colin was called to the desk, and given an address in Golden Square, which was the Luncheon Vouchers head office, where he picked up a parcel to deliver to Brixton. (*'Wow, Brixton,'* he *muttered*) He was given a 2/6p tip for his services. (*'Not bad he thought, getting half a crown for myself, and doing a job I really enjoy, he mumbled. I hope to get a few more of these Luncheon Voucher deliveries!*)

Colin met Lyn that evening, and they went to the Streatham Locarno, as he wanted to treat Lyn, due to receiving the 2/6p tip earlier that day. 'Not enough to get us both in, he thought, but at least I am with the girl I love.' They had a great evening and even managed to blag a couple of beers from an unsuspecting barmaid, who did not question their age.

They danced and spoke of their days at work, once they were seated; Lyn worked at the National Provincial Bank in Regent Street, but although Colin worked about ten minutes away, in Wimpole Street, their hours overlapped, so travelling to work, or meeting for lunch was not possible.

After working at Wimpole Street for over a year, and showing his superior's that he was capable of more than delivering telegrams, he was summoned to the Area Postmasters office, and asked if he wanted to work at the newly opened Sorting office in Rathbone Place, where his duties would include some clerical work and also, assisting the IB, (Investigation Branch/Post Office Police) with some further duties. Colin was excited, not only was this promotion and more money, he would also be gaining more knowledge, and would also be visiting other Sorting Offices.

Colin accepted the new position and was asked to report to a Supervisor at Rathbone Place, the following morning. He had arranged to meet Lyn that evening, and they celebrated his promotion, by going to the Streatham Odeon cinema, to watch the latest Clint Eastwood movie, "The Good, The Bad & The Ugly"; both of them commented after the movie, on how good it was. 'I could watch that all over again,' said Lyn, Colin agreed.

Next morning, Colin reported for duty at the reception desk, at the new Rathbone Place District Sorting Office, after he had travelled to Tottenham Court Road, rather than Oxford Circus, which he found was easier, as the Northern Line took him straight there from Tooting Bec underground station, without changing lines.

Walter Woods came downstairs in the lift and greeted Colin. 'My name is Wally Woods', he said, I will take you by lift to the upper offices and introduce you to your new work colleagues, who will advise you of your duties.' (*Colin laughed to himself, 'Wally Woods!'*)

An hour later, after meeting his new workmates, he was shown to the "Corridors of Power", where authorised personnel would wander along a corridor of blacked-out glass, so that they could check that nobody below, in the main sorting office, was stealing from any of the Queens Mail. *'One day my boy, we may let you walk along these corridors, and watch what is going on.'*

Wally Woods laughingly exclaimed. There was quite a lot to take on board on his first day, but Colin loved every minute and couldn't wait to tell Lyn, when he saw her next, during the week.

It was 10.00 am the next morning, and Colin had been asked to report to a Mrs. Bunty Jennings, a senior Clerical Officer, on the second floor, where he would be shown his next duty for the day. '*Call me Bunty darling*', she said. Colin was lost for words, he had never met such an overpowering woman like Bunty, but he was now part of a new team, and wanted to succeed in his new position. Bunty produced a black leather brief case, with the initials "ER" engraved in gold letters, just under the handle. Bunty asked Colin to give her his right wrist, and immediately handcuffed the case to it. *'Now darling, Bunty roared, take this case to King Edward Buildings (KEB) in King Edward Street, close to St Paul's underground station, where you will report to the security office and await further instructions!'* Colin hid his fear and thought about the James Bond films he had seen with Lyn. (*'Now I'm a spy,' he thought*)

Colin took the underground train to St Paul's station, he saw King Edward Buildings, once he was outside the station, and walked over to the security desk, where he was asked to follow a small stocky guard into a corridor; the guard tapped loudly onto a small wooden set of doors, which looked like a serving hatch. '*Yes, who is there*', a booming voice called out! *'Delivery from Western DO Sir!'* replied the guard. The man behind the voice asked Colin for his case, and produced a key, to remove it. *'Please wait in the room opposite son, called*

the man; and we will give you a case to take back'!
After ten minutes, Colin was called over to the hatch, where another brief case was handcuffed to his wrist.

He then returned to Rathbone Place, wishing he could tell someone about his "cloak and dagger" mission, but he remembered that he'd signed the Official Secrets Act!

Colin had dinner with his parents that evening and together they discussed his new position, with Colin stating that he was very happy with his new job, but was unable to say too much, due to being sworn to secrecy. 'Fulham are playing at home this Saturday, said his father, are you coming son?' 'Love to dad,' Colin replied.

It was Friday morning, and Colin wondered what tasks he was about to undertake that day; Wally Woods called him into the office and gave him an envelope, which contained some keys. 'You'll be working on the Post Office Railway today laddie, confirmed Wally Woods, and a word of warning son, *keep the keys safe, please!'*

Colin had never heard Wally shout, but knew the keys were of high importance.

'These keys are to be used to get you out, not in, just in case, do you understand?' Wally sounded different somehow, but Colin confirmed he understood. 'Now take the lift to the sub-basement laddie, and you will be met by a Mr. Peter White, who will take you to the underground areas below.' 'Thank you, Wally, I look forward to it,' Colin replied.

The lift seemed to take forever, but finally landed on the sub-basement level, where Peter White was waiting for him. 'Hi Colin, I'm Peter, call me Pete, and welcome to the Post Office Railway.' Peter White led Colin to a platform, where he spotted a small train, waiting on a narrow gauge set of rails. (*Wow, he thought, if only I could have smuggled my Instamatic camera down here!'*) 'Can you load those sacks onto the carriages please Colin, asked Pete, but only the sacks that are opposite the cabin doors please!'

Each sack was marked with its destination, but Colin checked before he threw the sacks, and carefully identified each one before he deposited them into the correct train carriages. He spotted some of the stations served, including Paddington, Wimpole Street, Mount Pleasant, King Edward Buildings, Liverpool Street and Whitechapel. He managed to load all the sacks into the small carriages, under the scrutiny of Pete, who commended him on being capable, and most of all, doing as he was asked to; the carriages were closed, then the small train started its journey west, towards its next stop, which was Wimpole Street.

Colin and his father attended the Fulham v Manchester City game, at the Craven Cottage ground that Saturday afternoon, with Fulham beating the away team by four goals to one. 'I need a drink son, lets pop into our local when we get back and I'll buy you a pint!' 'Thanks dad, said Colin, but I'm meeting Lyn about seven this evening, and wanted to get ready; some other time maybe?'

Lyn looked even more adorable that evening, and Colin couldn't wait until they were old enough to get engaged, but for now, he kept his thoughts to himself. They went to the cinema again, and this time, it was the Mayfair in Tooting, where they watched "Our Man

Flint", starring James Coburn; they both enjoyed the film but Lyn said she preferred the James Bond movies.

They wandered down to an Italian café, just past the cinema.in the direction of Tooting Broadway, and ordered some coffees. They spoke about their last few days, and many other subjects, and Lyn was so happy that Colin was enjoying his new career, even though he was unable to say too much about it.

It was Monday morning again, Colin reported to Wally Woods, and was asked to return to the Post Office Railway, once more, to join Peter White again, and was told that he would be working on his own for a few hours, due to someone calling in sick. 'Any problems son, just lift up the phone and ask for Wally,' Peter told the excited boy.

At Paddington Sorting Office, the small narrow-gauge train departed east, and headed for Wimpole Street, Colin could see the trains movements, by looking at the red neon lights on the screen behind him. 10 minutes later, he heard the sound of the train getting closer, it was travelling very fast, but it didn't stop at Rathbone Place; Colin suddenly vanished!

Above the sub-basement level, Peter White was sitting at a desk, which overlooked parts of the railway activity, and could see that there was a problem with one of the trains. He made his way down the stairs, as the lifts were, for some reason, out of order; he placed a code into the small square box outside the main entry door, and a red light came on. He then punched the six-figure code in once more and again, the red light showed. Peter picked up the handset by the side of the override push, which also didn't function, then pressed the red button. The button should have alerted the Control office, but there was no power at all. (*'Looks like we have a major power failure,' he thought*)

Peter heard some strange noises, and noticed that there were flashing lights, when he put his face close to a small gap in the door; which were coming from inside the station, but he couldn't get past the door, so he was unable to investigate any further.

Two hours later, the power came back, and both Peter White and Wally Woods accessed the main door to the platform. **'Colin, Colin, are you here?'** They got no response. They searched everywhere, even both ends of the tunnel entrances, but Colin was nowhere to be seen. 'Well, said Wally, he had keys to get out, but that door was electrically sealed, so where is he?' *'Looks like he has vanished into thin air,'* Stated Peter.

After contacting each adjoining station, there was no report of anyone seeing Colin, as they thought he may have somehow, fallen into one of the train carriages. Wally started to panic, he had never lost any employee under his watch, and tried to think about where Colin would have gone. (*'It's a total mystery,' he muttered.*) Peter told the excited boy.

The Investigation Branch (IB) were called in, and asked for written statements from everyone who worked on the railway, which would include their whereabouts that morning, up until the boy, known as Colin Parker, had suddenly vanished.

Two days later, after a lengthy search of all areas, and breaking the sad news to Colin's parents, they had no further clues to confirm what had taken place, as nobody had seen anything, so they had to assume the worst-case scenario.

Further investigations were carried out, over the next few days, and the current Postmaster General, Edward Short MP became personally involved.

Lynda Maberley was distraught after hearing the news about the disappearance of her boyfriend. Colin's mother explained to Lyn, by telephone, only what she knew, but was still awaiting further news from the GPO. They were both shedding tears after their discussion, and Lyn wondered what she could do. 'If they have not found Colin, we cannot make any further plans,' Lyn exclaimed.

Wally Woods attended an inquest over the incident and gave his account; he stated that this was the first time anything like this had happened, and had no idea where Colin had gone. He was then informed that the search had been called off, and that the only verdict they could apply to this, was Death by misadventure.

Lyn was grieving, and found it hard to get any sleep, when she was informed of the outcome of the GPO inquest, but finally, she managed to drift off into a deep slumber. She started to dream of Colin, she could see him, but could not make out where he was; he was speaking, but she couldn't hear him; all she could see was the small train, a tunnel and lots of flashing lights, then she could hear a voice speaking.

'Lyn, I was sucked into a vacuum, you must join me, you must get them to replicate the speeding train, then once you are here with me, they need to reverse the train, at the same speed, then we can both get back,

trust me darling, trust me!'

Lyn woke up the next morning, and wondered about the dream she had the night before. *'Was it a dream, or was it actually Colin calling out for help?'* she wondered. The more she thought about it, the more she wanted to talk to someone, to see if this was actually feasible.

Lyn contacted Wally Woods, after calling the Sorting Office at Rathbone Place. He listened, and told her he would call her back. Wally contacted Peter White, the Controller, who would be able to answer any questions. Peter confirmed that it was a long shot, however, they had a problem with the girl, as she was not a GPO employee, but Wally responded with a plan.

Lyn was picked up at the Sorting Office Reception, and signed in as a visitor, who would be assisting Peter White. Since Colins disappearance, the trains had been suspended, but after hearing the alleged details from Lyn, and agreeing to go ahead with it, the trains were reinstated, for tests only!

At Paddington Sorting Office, the small narrow-gauge train departed east at full speed, heading for Wimpole Street, Peter White watched the red neon lights on the screen; he also watched the lonely female figure on the platform below from a monitor, and hoped this would work. Peter told the excited boy.

The red neon lights started to fade, after each station had been passed, the train was getting faster, and overshot the Rathbone Place stop; Peter went down to check, but Lyn had vanished.

Peter White switched the controls into override, and

put the train into slow, then stop, when it had arrived at King Edward Buildings, in the city. He checked everything and put the reverse mode into play; the train started its return journey, on its way back to Paddington. The narrow-gauge train was now in full speed, it shot past all the stations, not stopping until it had arrived at Paddington Branch Office. Peter looked at his monitor, and saw two figures standing on the platform, holding hands.

Colin and Lyn were reunited and extremely happy with the outcome. Wally Woods and Peter White released them from the platform area, then alerted all the station controllers, to confirm that controls had been returned to its normal service, and that the Post Office Mail Train was functioning as normal.

After a quick briefing in Peter Whites Office, Wally Woods asked Lyn to sign a form, then confirmed to the couple that they could not tell anyone about what had happened.

'Remember, Peter said, you have both signed the Official Secrets Act!'

12: OUT OF THE SHADOWS

The British Airways passenger plane, touched down on time at Schiphol Airport, in Amsterdam. Four friends had planned this "boys-only" long weekend, using the time to frequent the local bars and pubs, in the lively areas of the town centre.

The train journey, from the Airport, would take about 15 minutes to arrive at Amsterdam Central, then a tram to Stadhouderskade, close to where they had booked two Airbnb, double rooms, adjacent to the canal and next door to the Heineken Brewery.

They quickly unpacked and made their way to one of the local bars, just across the square.

'Two pints of Amstel, a pint of Grolsch and a pint of Heineken please', asked Jim Randall. Jim had organised the trip, three-months ago; which was an annual get together, for each of the friends, where they would visit a new country, sample the local beers and have a good time.

The drinks arrived and were quickly swallowed; another round was asked for, together with some crisps. 'To soak up the alcohol', stated Bill Davies.

Jim Randall, Bill Davies, Kevin Townsend and Graham Frost, all worked for themselves, in the building industry. They met at their local pub most Sunday's, usually after a round of golf.

They met the "Spring Tavern", in Ewell, Surrey, a short walk from their homes in Stoneleigh and Ewell Village. They were all getting excited about their next trip, which was just two days away.

During their lunchtime session, they reminisced about the other long-weekend trips they had been to, including Prague, Barcelona, Cologne and Belfast; all of which were thoroughly enjoyed and when asked by their families, would state the trips were "Educational".

Three of the four mates had been married, but all these ended in divorce and costly settlements, due to the four children, they had between them. Now they lived for the annual city trip and the odd holiday to follow another passion, Formula One racing, across the world.

After unpacking their small cases and showering, they walked towards the town centre, to find Leidseplein Square, one of the city's most popular nightlife areas, home to famous music venues, fun dance clubs, relaxed bars and more.

They found a bar and ordered some drinks; Graham commented about the smell of the smoke and said it was making him feel woozy. 'Not what we are here for,' replied Jim.

They found an Indonesian restaurant, not too far from the bar and managed to get a table straight away.

They ordered sharing plates of Satay Chicken, Beef Rendang, roast chicken and lots of rice, together with four bottles of "Anker" beer.

More beers were ordered, together with another plate of Satay chicken. They paid the bill and walked back into the square. It was getting late, but the square was heaving. People of all nationalities were looking for the bars and restaurants; Jim was glad they had eaten earlier.

The following morning, after breakfast, Jim had arranged for a Canal Tour, in an open-top boat. They looked at the amazing sites and Bill Davies commented on some of the mid-terraced houses, that looked as if they were propping-up some of the others. 'We could make a fortune here lads,' exclaimed Kevin Townsend, 'Always thinking about work,' replied Jim.

'Time for some light refreshments everyone,' said Graham. They all agreed, as they alighted the open-top boat. They found the Hard Rock Café, overlooking the canal and ordered some Budweiser's, together with some light snacks. Graham again remarked on the smell of the smoke. 'Best we find another bar,' said Jim.

That evening, the four travellers found an Indian Restaurant, close to the notorious "Red-Light" district. They enjoyed the food and the copious bottles of Cobra beer.

They walked along the street, filled with bars, coffee shops' and the "skimpily-Clad" girls on show, behind the glass fronted shops. It was getting late, so Jim suggested they had another beer, before making their way back to the Airbnb.

The bar was quite packed, so they ordered some Amstel's and stood outside. Two attractive girls stood close by and Kevin started to chat to them. He found them very friendly and asked if they would like another drink. They thanked him and asked for a glass of white wine. Jim introduced himself to the girls and asked if they lived in Amsterdam. The girls confirmed that they rented an apartment with some other friends, close by, and would be here for another couple of days. Kevin returned with two glasses of wine.

Graham and Bill joined the conversation and one of the girls suggested they all come back to their place for a nightcap and to meet some of their friends. They finished their drinks and followed the girls to a narrow alleyway, then into a small hallway, with a lift. The elevator took them down a couple of floors and when the doors opened, they were confronted by five stocky men, each carrying a gun. 'What the hell is going on,' shouted Jim! One of the men pointed at a door and asked them to enter. By this time, the two girls had returned to the lift. 'We've been set up,' said Bill. *'Silence, do not speak, shouted one of the men. Just be quiet and do as you are told!'*

In the room, Jim and Bill were asked to follow one of the men, to an adjoining room; Kevin and Graham followed one of the others, to a separate room, with the guns pointing at their backs and an occasional prod, to make sure they did as they were asked. Once inside each of the rooms, the gunmen left and locked the doors behind them. 'Now what,' whispered Jim to Bill, what the hell have we let ourselves into!

Each of the rooms contained two beds and a bucket. There was also a sink, soap and a towel.

What seemed like hours later, the door to Jim and Bills room was unlocked. An armed man entered and told them to follow him. Kevin and Graham were standing outside, looking at their two other friends. Jim shrugged his shoulders and nodded his head, as if to say I don't know what is going on.

The two, armed men ushered them into a large dark room and asked them all to wait there until they were called. They heard the sound of the key turning the lock; they all sat down and wondered what was in store for each of them.

Jim whispered, 'sorry guys, I really don't know what is going on; I can only assume the two girls were the bait and we stupidly fell for it, sorry!' 'Had it not been for the gun's, whispered Graham, I am sure we could have taken them on!'

They heard a whirring noise and the dim lighting became lighter. They looked across, to the rear of the room and saw a small "rise and fall" door, slowly opening, revealing a smoky atmosphere; the smoke smelled the same as they had witnessed in the Hard Rock Café.

'*YOU*, said one of the armed men, pointing at Kevin. Follow me!' Kevin obeyed and walked over to the small doorway. '*GO*, go through and do as you are told!'

On the other side, Kevin found himself in what appeared to be an arena. He could see people inside, who were seated around a high wooden barrier, with mesh screening above. The barrier formed a circle, around the dusty floor, where Kevin stood. Then the lighting slowly dimmed.

Kevin panicked, he was sweating, he could hear something; something that did not sound human. He looked at the audience around him and saw that they were all men and amongst them, were the two girls from outside the bar.

Then, from out of the shadows, Kevin spotted a small grotesque creature. It was slimy, with pointed teeth, a large pot-belly, large pointed ears, long arms and stumpy legs. He wore only a loin-cloth and was restrained by a length of rope, around both his arms.

Kevin looked round, to see if he could find something to defend him, but he saw nothing. He looked up at the audience and noticed they were passing money to each of the girls, who gave them a receipt. To his left he saw an electronic screen, which showed the odds against a time and all he could imagine, was that how long he would last and the person who was closest would win the money.

A bell rang, the ropes binding the creature, loosened and fell to the ground. Kevin was a strong man and would fight the beast, but all he had was his fists. The beast went down on all four limbs and started to creep slowly over to the scared quarry. Kevin raised his fists in defiance.

Outside the room, the remaining three friends could hardly hear anything. Graham said he thought he could hear a crowd cheering and something that sounded like a growling dog. The three of them were no longer being guarded, so they looked around, to see if they could find a way out. It was futile, the room was empty.

All they could see, was the small doorway, where their friend Kevin had gone through, just over ten-minutes ago.

The beast was now breaking into a trot, using his four limbs to chase its prey. Kevin watched every move made by the grotesque animal and positioned himself with his back against the wooden barrier. The beast leapt high into the air and sank its teeth into Kevin's shoulder. The wound was deep and the crowd roared. Kevin grabbed one of the creature's arms and punched it hard, then threw him head-first into the barrier, to the delight of the crowd. The creature was stunned; Kevin placed his strong arms around the beast's neck and squeezed as hard as he could, until it stopped breathing.

Kevin was led out of the arena and taken to a room, where his wounds were dressed by a young girl.

She gave him a drink and some scraps of food. He recognised the girl who served him. 'Why, he asked, why did you bring us here!' The girl did not respond and left.

'*YOU*, called the armed man, you are next!' Bill Davies crawled through the opening and into the arena. He saw the crowds, the screen and the blood on the ground. 'What have you done to my friend,' he shouted! Just at that moment, he heard a roar; it sounded like a lion.

Then, once again, from out of the shadows, another beast appeared. It looked like a large dog, but its face was long and thick, more like a cross-bred Staffordshire Bull Terrier and an American Bulldog.

Bill saw that the creature had been restrained with ropes, but they were getting looser and starting to fall.

Bill didn't wait for the ropes to become any looser, he ran as fast as he could and landed a punch on its large nose. He then lay on top of the beast and kept landing punches all over its face. The creature was very strong and lifted itself up, throwing Bill onto the ground. It opened its large mouth and bit into Bills leg, then once he had released his grip, he sank his long sharp teeth into Bills neck; Bill passed out and laid on the ground, with blood oozing fast, from each of his wounds. The beast was shot with a tranquilising dart, then four large men appeared.

They dragged away both the lifeless bodies out of the arena, to the cheers and boos from the audience.

Graham and Jim heard the shouts and cheers from behind the entrance and wondered how Kevin and Bill had done; then in walked an armed man.

'*YOU* and *YOU*, both of you, he called out, go through!'

Both friends did as they were told, then, once they were through the access door, they saw the audience of men. Graham pointed to the screen, which showed a green tick and a red cross. Jim saw the blood, and asked Graham to stand behind him, and do as he was told.

'Hopefully, Jim said, whatever they send out to fight us, will be over quickly, but we cannot go down without a fight!'

The crowd roared, as they saw what was coming out of the shadows, there were two beasts!

Both creatures again, were cross-bred, very stocky, Staffordshire Bull Terriers, which were loosely tied, but they were pulling and biting their restraints; these beasts were hungry, and were looking at the two figures, who stood ten-yards away.

'Hope my Martial Arts training will help us, stated Jim. As I said Graham, keep behind me and wait until they make their move!'

The ropes dropped away and both the creatures ran towards their prey; Jim stooped forward and cupped his hands together.

Just as the first beast pounced, Jim grabbed its body and threw it as hard as he could. The creature was thrown over the mesh screen and landed into the audience. Screams were heard, when the beast started biting and tearing at the limbs, of those who had fallen, in the panic.

The other creature sensed that something was wrong, but being hungry, it circled both figures, looking for a way to use its razor-sharp teeth, to tear into the flesh and kill the targets.

Graham was caught off guard, the beast had managed to bite into his leg, so Jim turned round and grabbed the creature by its neck and started punching its face, continually but it wouldn't let go. Graham screamed in pain, but his adrenaline gave him some extra strength, so he grabbed one of the creature's front legs, and snapped it; which made the beast release his grip from Grahams legs.

The crowd were still trying to get to the exits, but the other beast was still biting, and tearing into whoever they could; one of them was a girl.

Jim saw that the creature was in agony, but managed to grab its rear legs; Graham assisted by grabbing the front legs and together, the beast was thrown over the mesh screen, to more screams from the remaining audience.

'Now we need to find Bill and Kevin,' shouted Jim! Graham grabbed Jim's shoulder, as a support, then limped across the arena. Eventually, they found a corridor, behind the entrance, of which the two dogs had come through.

They heard yelping, loud barks, and the odd roar, but spotted that each of the animals were caged. One of the gunmen, who had ushered each of them into the arena, lay on the floor; his throat had been ripped away, leaving a large pool of blood all around him. Kevin Townsend appeared, he was bandaged and spots of blood were showing through the dressing. 'Follow me, said Kevin to his two friends. Sorry guys, Bill didn't make it!'

'Ok said Jim, let's just get the hell out of this place, so that we can get some help!' The three of them found the lift and used it, to transport them up a couple of floors, then into the narrow alley, they had come through earlier.

There were several police cars and ambulances outside an office block, at the end of the alleyway, which they later found out, was the main entrance to the arena. A policeman spotted the three figures emerging from the side alley, and called a paramedic over, to check out their injuries. The medic took one look at their wounds, so the ambulance took them to a local hospital.

Jim Randall gave the detective, a full account of their ordeal, then the officer confirmed that they had been trying to find the leaders of what started as an illegal "Dog-Fighting" ring, which has now involved unsuspecting human beings, for monetary gain.

'We are sorry for the death of Mr. Davies, said the officer, we have already contacted the British Embassy in the Hague, and they will arrange for the deceased to be flown back to the UK.'

The detective thanked them for their assistance in the matter and confirmed that a number of arrests had been made.

The flight back was depressing for the three friends. They arrived home, and arranged to meet in the Spring Tavern that evening. The locals looked at the three wounded friends and someone commented on what must have been a great long-weekend, but he got no response.

The barman asked what they would like to drink. Jim asked for three pints of Pravha. The barman confirmed that the Pravha was finished, and would they like Amstel instead. '*Definitely Not,*' replied all three of them!

13: SCRIBBLE

The document baffled the investigating police officer; it was an official looking agreement, between the deceased person, and someone else, but one of the names on the paperwork was illegible, just a piece of scribble.

The police officer did some research on the dead person, who was named as James Turner, aged 44, single and who lived in Harley Mews, in the West end of London.

Jim Turner was a doctor, specialising in psychiatry, and had an office in Harley Street, famous for its doctors. Jim worked long hours and as his fees were paid by the hour, he was extremely rich. He owned the mews house, close to his office, and had properties in Berkshire and France, all paid for by his profession; he dated occasionally, but due to his long working hours, didn't want anything permanent.

Jim took a well-earned break for 2-weeks and spent it in Nice, staying at one of his properties. He often visited the casinos of Monte Carlo, only if he was on holiday, and sometimes, gambled vast amounts of money, which attracted all sorts of people, who would watch him.

Jim wasn't a sociable type, where money was concerned, he knew by experience, what people would do, to get their hands on it, so he kept himself to himself, and walked away, if he suspected anybody being intrusive.

He won several thousand Euros at the "Casino de Monte Carlo", that evening, and decided to spend the night in one of the 47 rooms, after drinking a few to many large scotches. He called room-service, and ordered some sandwiches and coffee, to soak up the alcohol, which was delivered ten minutes later, by an elderly waiter, who looked about eighty years old. (*'Must be the long hours, Jim thought to himself?'*)

He gave the waiter 100 Euro's, and thanked him for the prompt service, the waiter was ecstatic with the tip and couldn't thank him enough, and confirmed that he was just finishing his long shift. They spoke briefly and discussed why the waiter was still working, due to his age.

'I am fifty-two years of age,' confirmed the waiter.

'Please accept my apologies,' replied Jim.

The waiter explained that he aged quickly, since he had worked at the casino, but couldn't understand why. 'Maybe something to do with my gambling addiction,' he said, with a sad look in his eyes.

'Maybe I can help,' stated Jim, I am a psychiatrist. Maybe a few minutes with me, I may be able to help your addiction; and at no cost of course!'

The waiter thanked him again and asked if he had a few minutes after he had signed off from his shift. Jim agreed and asked his name.

'Martin Ammon,' replied the waiter. Martin returned fifteen minutes later, and sat opposite James Turner. The usual questions were asked; how much do you spend, are you in debt etc. Martin gave positive responses to all the questions and was asked if he minded being hypnotised.

Under his hypnotic state, Jim had made sure that Martin wouldn't gamble anymore, and should he be tempted to use his money to bet on anything, he would feel a short shock inside him, that would deter him.

Martin came out of the trance and told Jim he couldn't remember anything about being hypnotised. He then thanked the doctor and left the room.

Jim returned to Nice and continued with his holiday; he sat in a beach bar, overlooking the Mediterranean Sea, sipping a Vodka-Martini, when he spotted Martin Ammon walking past. He called out to him and asked him if he wanted to join him for a drink. Martin acted surprised and said he was visiting his sister close by.

They had a quick chat and Jim asked Martin if he wanted to meet him at a local casino that evening. Martin declined the offer and said he hoped they would bump into each other soon.

The day before Martin was due to fly back home, he had a drink with Martin and asked him
how he was doing. Martin said he couldn't understand why he wouldn't go into a casino, but thanked Jim, for his help.

'If there is ever anything I can do for you Doctor Turner, please don't hesitate to call me, and left a hand written mobile number on the table.

Jim looked at the scrap of paper and although he could read the number, he couldn't make head or tail of the scribble by it, so he placed the sheet into his pocket and waved goodbye to his new friend.

Jim was back to work the day after returning, and waded through all the paperwork and promptly swished the desk with his arm and then checked his voicemails. '*Nothing of interest here,*' he muttered.

That evening, he met some friends for dinner in Chinatown; he loved Chinese food and the ambience of the restaurants. They finished and paid for the dinner, and two of his friends asked him if he wanted to join them for an after-dinner drink. Jim agreed and they made their way to a casino close by, where Jim won a couple of hundred pounds on the roulette table and a few more on the poker game. He suddenly thought to himself about Martin, but agreed he was not an addict, as he knew when to stop.

Over the course of the next few weeks, Jim had lost thousands of pounds in different London casinos, but still convinced himself that he was not "Hooked". '*Well not yet, he thought, but I must be careful.*'

After almost a year, Jim had managed to spend most of his savings in the casinos and had taken out a second mortgage on his cottage in Harley Mews.

He tried to stop, but something inside him, made him want to play the poker and roulette tables, so he was going downhill fast!

In his Harley Street office one morning, he received a call from Martin Ammon, asking him if he would like to meet up for dinner, as he was over from France for a few days. Jim accepted and they met in the Ritz Hotel in Piccadilly. Over dinner, Jim told Martin of his problems and asked him how he was doing these days.

'Everything ok thanks to you Jim. I have saved sufficient money to open a Restaurant, near my sister's place in Nice, so cheers to you, my friend. Martin asked how Jim how he was doing; Jim responded with *'not too well unfortunately.'* They discussed Jim's gambling addiction, and his lack of funds lately; due to the amounts of money he was spending.

'You kindly helped me Jim, stated Martin, so let me help you. I will sort out the bill and meet you upstairs in the lounge bar.' Jim felt embarrassed for once in his life; he was the one that should be helping people to overcome their problems and now he was the one, asking for help. Martin arrived and asked Jim if he would like to get back on his feet again, but would need to stop the gambling, once he revealed his offer of help.

'Anything, just get me out of this mess, ***please***!' Stated Jim.

They arranged to meet the following evening, at the Dorchester Hotel in Park Lane.

Over dinner Martin confirmed that he would make Jim a partner in his new business, with a fifty-percent share, just for helping him, when he had *his* gambling problems. Jim agreed and thanked Martin, who said he would draw up the paperwork.

They met again, at a pub near Jim's mews house, in London, and sat in a quiet place at the rear. Martin produced a document, of which Jim read, and agreed to sign. He wrote his signature at the bottom of the contract, and Martin signed his name underneath Jim's.

Martin confirmed to Jim that he would get the document registered and would send him a copy in due course.

A week later, Jim checked his bank details and noticed that a large sum of money had been credited to his account, dated the day after he had signed the contract. He breathed a sigh of relief and made a list of his debts, which he wanted to pay off as soon as possible.

Martin contacted Jim, to ask whether he had received the credit in his bank account; Jim couldn't thank his new business partner enough, and confirmed that he was gradually going to pay off all his debts.

That afternoon, Jim had hypnotised one of his patients, who had some problems with drug addiction and gambling. This was the patients fourth session, and after coming out of his trance, was informed that he should now be able to get on with his life, without the drugs and gambling dependencies.

Knowing that he went through the same problems, Jim suggested that they go to a casino in London, to see if the treatment had been successful.

Later that afternoon, Jim and his patient went to a club in Park Lane, Mayfair. Jim went to the bar for some drinks, and watched as his patient hovered around the roulette, poker tables and slot machines, but his patient showed no interest whatsoever and thanked his doctor for helping him.

'Remember, said Jim, what you have just done, shows that you are on the road to full recovery, but you must resist any further temptations with gambling or drugs, or everything I have done, will be wasted!'

Jim's patient finished his drink and left. The barman asked Jim if he wanted another drink, as he was about to settle his tab; he thanked him and asked for a large scotch and soda.

As he slowly sipped the drink, he looked across at the slot machines, checked his pockets for some loose change, and thought to himself. *"I suppose one little flutter won't hurt"*?

An hour later, Jim had changed over a hundred pounds into change for the slot machines. This then led to several wagers on the roulette wheel, where he managed to lose more money; his addiction had returned!

Jim was invited over to Nice, to join Martin and check on his 50% investment of the restaurant, and Jim was flabbergasted, as the place was packed.

He noticed at least six waiters and two waitresses, serving drinks and food to the attending customers. Martin introduced Jim to most of the staff and led him to a quiet table, and ordered a bottle of the 2005 Chateau Mouton Rothschild and two glasses.

'How is everything Jim, asked Martin; have you managed to overcome the gambling addiction?'

'Of course, my dear friend, thanks to you, replied Jim. I have moved on with my life and have sorted out the important debts, and, look at this fine restaurant which you kindly gave me a half-share; for that, I will be always be eternally grateful!'

Martin gave Jim a look, but Jim failed to notice that the glaring eyes were red!

'Just one minor thing Jim, asked Martin. Did you receive the copy of the contract; I ask because I wanted to make sure that you kept it safe, in case of any legalities that you must declare?'

Jim confirmed that the document was in a safe at his office in Harley Street, so Martin asked whether he had any questions over the wording of the document, but Jim confirmed that he had read the words, when he saw it, and had signed it. Martin raised his glass and "chinked" Jim's, then together, both said, 'Salut!'

On the plane back home, Jim started to think about his conversation with Martin, regarding the wording on their contract. *'He was just being cautious he thought.'*

Jim had just finished a session with a patient and checked his appointments for the rest of the day; his next one would be in an hour, so he made a coffee and sat down. He looked across at his safe and wondered about the Contract, and opened the safe, then removed it. He sipped a mouthful of the coffee and perused the terminology and gasped!

"Should you indulge in the activities you were involved with, prior to signing this document, then you will forfeit everything you have been given, together with your existence". ***'These words have been changed!'*** He shouted.

He started to panic, but wondered whether Martin would know about his recent visit and money losses at the casino in Park Lane. *'I doubt it.'* He hoped!

His next patient arrived; a man, who was a new patient, and was quite wealthy looking, and when Jim asked about his problem, the man stated, '*YOU!*'

Jim stood up and asked his patient what he meant. The man said he knew about Jim's gambling and that he was sworn, on oath, that he would not resort to his previous indulgencies and would therefore, be bound to the terms of the document in his safe. 'How would you know this,' asked Jim. 'I know about everything, I have watched you since the day you signed the contract, so, in accordance with the document you have signed, you must now forfeit you're your life!'

James Turner found himself in a hospital bed, connected to a life-support machine; a nurse came in and checked him over, but he was dead! His soul was now in possession by the man known as Martin Ammon.

The police officer asked one of his colleagues to see if he could decipher the signature on the document that had been found in the safe, belonging to the deceased. The colleague was a Forensics Officer, whose expertise was in Cryptology, so he studied the document, and then the signatures, with his magnifying glass and confirmed what he had found. 'The document is bona-fide and was signed by the deceased, known as James Turner. The witnesses "scribbled" signature was M Ammon.'

The police officer checked his records, but couldn't find anything. The forensics officer returned and confirmed that he had checked the name. '*MAMMON*, he said, is related to *"The Seven Princes of Hell"*, so maybe, this could, if you believe in the old scriptures, and ancient writings, would have been a "Deal with the Devil"?

175

14: SYMBOLS

After a long night of drinking at a local hostelry in Padstow, Cornwall, four good friends, who had travelled down from South London, to spend a few days relaxing, had discussed possibly searching for buried treasure, as one of many activities, over the short time. Some of them had read about the stories about pirates, who had allegedly landed at some of the beaches, who had buried their ill-gotten gains, close to where they moored.

It was a warm sunny morning the next day, and after a large "English" breakfast, Tom, Rick, Martin and James, started their quest, by driving towards Perranporth, which was less than an hour's drive away. They were armed with a map, two metal detectors, some shovels and quite a few cases of lager.

All four of the guys worked in the City of London, either in banking or for the Stock Exchange. They told all their friends, that they worked hard, and played even harder, and had done the usual parachute jump, the mountain climbing, and other dangerous sports, so the long weekend in Cornwall, was a "chill-out" time for them, so a treasure hunt was ideal.

They found a small pub on the outskirts of Perranporth, and stopped for a "swift-half", before they started their search, and found that the landlady was very friendly, when she made conversation with the lads, asking them what they were doing in the area. Tom explained that they were probably going on a treasure hunt in the area, but also confirmed that they had no experience, so any help would be welcome.

A small bearded man appeared from the adjoining bar and, in a broad Cornish accent, offered to be of assistance, so they asked him if he would like a drink, and if they could join him in the "snug". The barmaid poured a pint of "Doombar" for the man, knowing that this was his regular drink.

'I be George Davey, he said, you be looking at the old fairground close to the Methodist Church on Ponsmere

Road.' He then produced a local map, and pointed out the Church. 'Yertiz', he exclaimed!

Tom gave him a ten-pound note for his time and thanked him, George was very thankful to the four strangers from London, so he gave them the map, and suggested they start their search, about 200 yards west from the Church, with the old oak tree to their right. 'Has anyone else found anything in this area,' James asked, with an inquisitive look.

'Aye, the odd bit of gold and other items has been found here, stated George Davey. The four friends smiled and wondered whether he was telling them the truth?

'This place was very popular with the pirates back in the old days, continued George. it was due to being so close to the sea, and there could still be a lot more treasure somewhere; oh, and just one more thing lad's, there were rumours of curses being buried with some of the treasures, curses that have made people disappear!'

They found the Methodist Church on Ponsmere Road and parked the car close by. 'What was that old guy rambling on about, asked James, curses, and people disappearing?'

Everyone chuckled, and started walking away from the Church, trying to look for a good spot, about 200 yards away. After switching on their Metal Detectors, they heard the odd bleep, and started their digging in two separate spots, where they managed to find a few old "Pre-Decimal" coins, plus four ring pulls. 'Not a lot going on here called out Martin, why don't we check out some other spots?'

Back in the pub, the landlady spoke to George Davey, and asked him why he had mentioned the curses, but George responded, saying he was delighted with the ten-pound tip and that these boys needed to know about the strange things that had happened to other treasure hunters over the years. 'But nothing has ever been proved she said, and yes, there were reports of missing persons, but the local Constabulary stated that these were just rumours, to keep any treasure hunters away from Perranporth!'

Rick watched the metal detectors being swayed left and right over the grassy areas, and made himself useful, by tidying up the loose areas, where the soil had been removed. He used a small trowel, and returned the earth back to normal, he then shovelled out a small amount of mud, in an adjacent patch and felt something solid below. He investigated further, and saw a piece of wood, so he frantically widened the aperture, which revealed what looked like a wooden chest, and called out to his three friends. 'Better come over here chaps, looks like I have found something!'

Tom ran one of the metal detectors over the wooden box, but there was no bleeping. James started carefully digging a wider hole around the box, then dug down deeper, on each side, until the entire chest was revealed. Two of the guys carefully lifted the casket, and both remarked on how heavy it was. The loose soil was replaced and tidied, to make it look like it hadn't been touched, then they carried the chest over to their car, and placed a blanket over it. Everyone looked around, to make sure they were not being watched, but couldn't see anybody in the area.

'Lunch is calling chaps, called Tom, let's find somewhere, a short drive away from Perranporth, then we can discuss how and what we can do with our find, once we look inside the chest!'

They drove a few miles back on the road they had taken earlier from Padstow and stopped at a pub called the Falcon Inn, in a place called St Mawgan. 'Perfect chaps, said Tom, they have a restaurant here, so let's go and eat!'

They managed to get a table overlooking the Car Park, so that they were able to keep an eye on their car; and also, the wooden box under the blanket! Over lunch, they agreed that they would find a deserted spot somewhere on the way back to Padstow, so that they could open the chest without being noticed.

They found an ideal place, where they saw a small area, with trees, after driving again on the road back to Padstow; four very excited friends couldn't wait to open the wooden casket. Rick and James picked up the chest and looked for a lock, but they couldn't see one, they looked for an opening, or any way of getting inside, but there was nothing that would allow them to access the interior of the large box. 'Use the spade, shouted Tom, break the damn thing open, we are growing very impatient chaps!'

The box split open after several attempts; they all looked inside and gasped, when they saw two golden chalices, some diamond necklaces, gold coins, rings and lots of silver items. Tom picked up a sheet of paper from inside the chest lid, which he turned over, and saw some symbols, so he folded the paper and placed it into his coat pocket. *'Not sure what those symbols mean, he thought to himself, maybe they could lead us to other treasure?'*

They placed the chest back in the boot, covered it with the blanket, then took the road back to the hotel.

That evening, they went to Rick Stein's Seafood restaurant by the harbour, which Tom had booked several months ago; the food, the wine and the ambience were first class, and they all agreed that it was a brilliant choice. A visit to the Harbour Inn just around the corner was also a good idea, it had been an amazing day, but they still had to work out, what to do with the chest of treasure.

Over a nightcap at their hotel, they decided to contact the local museum the next morning, to make sure they were not accused of trying to steal anything, and Tom hoped that the symbols he had found, could be deciphered.

Mr Wright, the curator of Padstow Museum, met Tom and Rick the next morning, after they had spoken to him.

Tom explained what they had found, and showed Mr Wright a number of photos from his mobile, but Mr Wright said they should have reported the find to the police first, although he agreed that he would take care of it. 'Well done boys, exclaimed an excited Mr Wright, you have found something that until now was thought to be a myth!' Tom and Rick looked at each other, wondering how much this "Myth" was worth!

'Hopefully, you didn't find any papers in the chest, said Mr Wright, please tell me you didn't!'

Tom produced the single sheet he had found inside the chest, and suddenly, the colour drained from Mr

Wright's face. 'W-who have you shown this to,' he asked. Tom confirmed that only he had seen the symbols, but felt the anxiety coming from the Museum Curator, and wondered what these symbols meant?

'Did anyone other than you touch the paper, Tom, asked the curator?'

'No, replied Tom, why, what is going on here, what do these symbols mean?'

Mr Wright explained that a witch's curse was buried with the treasure, and that anyone who looked at the symbols would die, or be cursed forever. The only way to break the curse, was to pass the paper to somebody else, then they would inherit the curse.

'When did you look at the symbols Tom,' asked Mr Wright?

'It was about 11.00 yesterday morning, why, he replied, what does the time I looked at these characters mean?'

'It means that the curse will commence at midnight, the following day,' confirmed a shaking Mr Wright!

Tom looked very worried and asked, 'How do I get out of this predicament Mr Wright, who can I give this paper to, please help me!'

The curator stated that it was his own fault for looking at the symbols, and said he must think carefully before passing them over to an unsuspecting person.

'I need to resolve this,' stated a trembling Tom, so they told Mr Wright, that they would get the chest over to him as soon as possible, and left the museum.

'What the hell am I going to do now Rick' asked Tom, I have until midnight tonight, to find someone to pass these symbols to!'

'Why don't we just go into a pub and pick someone out, stated Rick; then say is this yours?' 'Great idea Tom replied, let's go to the Harbour Inn, and hope they are open for business?'

The Inn was closed, but they spotted an old gentleman outside the pub and asked him what time they opened; the old man turned round; it was George Davey. '*You*' shouted Tom!

'Sorry lads, George said, I knows what ye are thinking, but I do not want the paper you have found!'

'How did you know we were in Padstow George; you were in Perranporth?' George gave them a quizzical look, then replied.

'You wanted to find the treasure boys, I gave you the clues, you found the treasure, but the curse has already commenced; someone must depart this earth at Midnight, good luck!' George Davey had an evil smirk on his wrinkled face, as he spoke.

Tom and Rick thought about the situation, and of George Davey, who must have known what would happen, once they had found the treasure. They heard the creak of the pub doors opening, and once they had ordered their drinks and found a seat, Tom asked George Davey what it would cost to get out of the witch's curse.

George looked at Tom, and said he would accept £500, then he would be able to help. Tom agreed, and asked George to wait for him at the pub, confirming that he would withdraw the cash from an ATM; and would get back in about 15 – 20 minutes.

Tom returned and passed ten £50 notes over to George Davey. 'Thankee lad, said George, ye will not be sorry!'

Tom, Rick, Martin and James had left Padstow and

were on their way back to South London. 'I don't trust that old guy, exclaimed Rick, he was so shifty, but how do you know you will not suffer at midnight mate?'

'Don't worry Rick, just wait till he counts out the money, he will find a piece of paper tucked inside the money, which has the symbols on it!'

Later that evening, George Davey counted out the ten, £50 pound notes, then his face dropped, as he looked around, waiting to see who, or what was coming to get him!

15: LIFEBLOOD

'Nurse, I have finished here, stated the surgeon, can you please check the sutures and give the patient a good clean up?'

The young nurse, named Jane, did as she was told and prepared the male patient for his short trip to the recovery room, once the other members of staff had completed their final checks and ensured that all the equipment used was placed into the sterilisers.

It was 30th July 1966, a date that most people will remember, as the day the FIFA World Cup Final, which would be played at Wembley Stadium, where England would play against West Germany.

Wembley Stadium was packed that day, with a combined total of 93,000 English and West German supporters. Those who were unable to get a ticket for this historic football match, had to watch it, from their black and white televisions.

During the match, the streets of the UK were mostly empty, except for the people who were not soccer fans.

In the sky above Wembley Stadium, a "cloaked" vessel hovered around the area and then
made its way at light-speed, across London and the surrounding suburbs, checking on activity below and looking for a quiet place to land their craft.

The operation at St James Hospital, in Balham was a success and the patient was slowly beginning to open his eyes. After some checks on his blood pressure and temperature, he was transferred to a ward, where he would spend approximately one week, after his Hiatus Hernia operation.

The spacecraft had scanned the inhabitants of the hospital below them and one of the crew beamed down to an empty room, within the Nurses Home. The alien had altered his shape and appearance, to look like a human male. He dressed himself with some clothes that had been copied and reproduced on their advanced technical equipment.

Jane Clarke had just finished her shift, she had started the previous evening at 8pm and due to the urgent operations in the hospital, finished at 10am the following morning. She made her way across to the Nurses Home, ready to catch up on some sleep and hopefully, to catch the World Cup Match, later that day.

The Alien heard someone in the corridor and then the sound of a key being placed in to the door lock. He made himself invisible and waited to see who would enter the room.

Jane couldn't be bothered with a shower, or eat, she just wanted to sleep. She closed the dark curtains, removed her uniform and slipped into her bed, and drifted off within minutes.

The space traveller watched silently and disappeared from the room, then made his way over to the hospital building.

After checking the wards and other parts of the hospital, he found what he was looking for; an operating theatre. He watched with interest, as the surgeons carried out their skilled craft, with the sharp scalpels cutting their way into the flesh of the patient, the blood seeping from the wound and the bag of blood dripping slowly, to replace the loss of blood, due to the operation.

He had seen enough. He now needed to report back to his crew and relate his findings to them and then, to carry out what they had come to the Planet Earth to do, to offer the human race something that would change their lives forever.

Jane Clarke woke up after managing to grab four hours sleep. She used the loo and ran a hot bath. The fridge was empty, except for a few eggs, some spam and a bottle of gold-top milk. She sat in the bath for over twenty minutes, dried herself and went back to the fridge. She made herself an omelette and a cup of tea, then switched on the TV, to catch the World Cup final.

She had missed the first half-hour of the match and had missed the goals as scored by each side, making it 1-1 at half-time. The game continued and after 90 minutes, the scores were level at 2-2.

'Extra time Jane thought to herself, but I must think about this evening at the Locarno in Streatham with the girls later. Plenty of time,' she sighed.

England beat West Germany 4-2, at the end of the extra time. The crowds were going mad, the England side were dancing around the pitch and made their way up to the Royal Box, where the Captain, Bobby Moore and his team, were awarded the "Jules Rimet" trophy and a winner's medal each, by Queen Elizabeth.

Jane's eyes were heavy, she fell asleep. She did not hear the Alien return to her room. He knew Jane worked in the hospital and somehow, he would need to discuss why he was on Earth and his intentions.

At the Locarno venue, later that evening, Jane and four of her close friends danced away, to a band called the Kinks, who currently had some chart success. They played some of their recent chart singles, including "Sunny Afternoon" and "Dead End Street". The girls thoroughly enjoyed the evening and Jane, together with a fellow nurse, caught a bus and a train, back to the hospital, in Balham.

The alien heard Jane return to her flat, at the Nurses home. He watched as she boiled the kettle and made herself a cup of coffee.

He didn't want to frighten her, so he had to think of a way of making contact, so that he could ask her to assist him in his quest. While she was away, he had searched her flat for any clues, so that he could make conversation.

Jane had a lie-in the next morning, as she was not working today.

She decided to go and get some shopping and walked to the local shops in Bellview Road, opposite Wandsworth Common, unaware that she was being followed.

The alien stood next to her, as she purchased some fruit from the greengrocers. He bumped into her as she turned around, ready to exit and apologised. 'Jane, is that you,' said the alien. 'Yes, she said, but sorry, I don't know you?'

'We were at Haselrigge Junior school together, I am Philip Glass!' The alien had hoped his research would remind Jane of her early schooldays in Clapham, and as she was now 19 years old, she wouldn't recognise his face.

'You must remember Mr James, the Headmaster, and Mr Soanes, his deputy, asked the alien.

Jane did remember the teachers, but Philip Glass, who she had a slight crush on, back then, was it really him? 'Of course, Jane replied, but it has been quite a few years since we were at Haselrigge; how could you recognise me, after all this time?'

'I cannot forget the pretty girl who sat next to me, all those years ago, tell me, what have you been up to, since we left school?'

Jane was happy to speak and wondered whether it was too forward, asking Philip if he fancied a drink. 'I would enjoy that,' stated the alien.

They walked up to the Surrey Tavern, on the corner of Bellevue Road and Trinity Road. Jane was a regular here, but was normally accompanied by her female friends, not a boyfriend.

The alien asked Jane to take a seat, and what she would like to drink. He ordered her a Gin and Tonic, and after looking round to see what the men in the bar were drinking, asked for a pint of Bitter.

They spoke about Jane working as a Junior Nurse at the hospital and of the aliens (*Now Philip Glass*) employment, to which he confirmed he was a Haematologist.

After another drink, Jane felt more at ease and as there were no boyfriends on the scene, hoped they could meet again.

They left the Surrey Tavern and went for a stroll across Wandsworth Common; Jane couldn't believe her luck, actually finding someone, someone she fancied along time ago at her junior school.

The alien had completed his first part of the mission, by gaining Jane's attention; now he had to think of a way to gain her trust, and confirm why he was visiting her planet. It was not going to be easy!

Jane didn't want the day to end, but she would need to get some sleep in a few hours, ready for an early shift, the following day. 'Can we meet again,' asked Philip?

'I would love to, replied Jane, why don't we meet again on Thursday, as I have two of days off?' The alien agreed and took her number.

Thursday was quite sunny, they had spoken by telephone; something that the alien was not too familiar with, and thinking about how communication was so dated on Earth.

They met outside the Surrey Tavern, at lunchtime, then ended up in London, after picking up a train at Wandsworth Common Station.

They "window-shopped" in Oxford Street, had a light lunch in the Lyons Corner House, on the corner of Park Lane, then strolled across to Hyde Park.

Jane threw some scraps of bread she had kept from their lunch, to a few pigeons, then thirty or more pigeons arrived!

'Jane, said Philip, I am so happy we have become friends, tell me, what are your plans with your career as a Nurse?'

Jane confirmed that one day, she wanted to be a doctor or a surgeon, but would need to study and enrol at college, only if I can afford it?

'I can help you, replied the alien, I have a way that will make you very famous, and will result in a career that everyone will be queueing up to offer you a job!'

Jane wondered what this was all about, a junior Nurse being offered a new career, and being famous. It sounded too good to be true. 'How?' asked Jane. 'I have not been honest with you Jane; I am not Philip Glass, I have been sent to Earth, to ask for help, as my species are dying. We need...'

'*Stop,* Jane shouted, what do you mean, sent to Earth, my species, what are you trying to tell me?'

'Please, let me continue, I will explain why I am here, and if you want me to go, I will!'

'I come from a planet, a long way from your earth, we have evolved over many centuries, but one day, our species started to become ill, and we lost many of our population.'

Jane was not amused at being duped, and being told he was an alien from another planet, but she went along with the story, as she wanted the answers to so many questions, but fearing what he might do, she continued to listen to him.

'We have perfected ways of travelling around the universe in seconds, we can assume any shape or form when required, and have everything we need, but with our race dying of an unknown disease, we do not have the ability to save them.'

Jane started to feel sorry for the alien, but wanted to understand what he actually wanted. The alien continued. 'Many of our species were sent to different planets, to check whether we could find ways to heal our dying race. One day, one of our kind was on course to your planet earth, and noticed a large spacecraft floating aimlessly above the planet you have named the moon. He entered the craft and noticed that the three people on board, were barely alive, due to a malfunction with their equipment. We later understood that some debris had collided with the Space Station, causing injury to one of the astronauts and the remaining two having serious injuries.

The astronaut had lost a lot of blood and our envoy gave him a single drop of his body fluid, which you call blood, although our blood is green. Within minutes, the astronaut was alive and well.'

'I can see now what you are trying to tell me, said Jane, but I have to ask what happened to this astronaut, did he return to earth and was he checked by his medical team?'

'The astronaut didn't see our envoy, and the single drop of green blood turned red, once it had entered his bloodstream. The tests he received showed nothing, so there was no evidence that he would have died, but it was too late to save the other two astronauts, as their injuries were fatal.'

'Ok said Jane, so what you're are saying, is that one drop of your blood can save a dying person; I get that, but what do you want in return'

'As I said before, stated the alien, we are a dying race, and the disease that is killing our people needs to be checked against the symptoms and possible cures that the earth people had been dying from, over many years.'

Jane asked the alien to explain how she would be able to help, knowing that she was only a junior nurse, and with no expertise in any of the diseases of the human race.

'I realise that this is all sounding like a far-fetched story to you said the alien, but I can show you something that will confirm who I really am!'

He looked around the area; there was nobody in the immediate vicinity. He asked Jane to close her eyes and hold onto his arm. They disappeared together and reappeared in a large space craft, with two other occupants staring at her. The alien had changed back to his normal shape; Jane wanted to scream, but what good would that do, she thought?

The alien then returned back to Hyde Park with Jane, after he had returned to his human body shape, as Philip Glass.

'Ok said Jane, now I believe you, but as I said before, how can I introduce your blood to our scientists, without being questioned over its origin and healing powers?'

'I am prepared to stay on earth and assist you over this replied the alien, you can become my assistant and together, we can convince your scientists of its healing properties and, at the same time, I will be able to gain the information over your diseases that have been successfully cured, over the last twenty years.'

Jane was happy to go along with the plan and after discussing the way forward, she gave a week's notice to St James Hospital.

Three months later, Jane and Philip had won the approval of the leading scientists, after the single drop of green liquid had been tested, and proved to be a cure for most red and white blood-cell disorders. Also, the liquid had managed to eradicate minor cancer cells. The new treatment was proving to be a worldwide success, and Jane was fast becoming a wealthy and celebrated scientist.

Philip Glass had researched the many diseases that had evolved over time with the human race and had entered all the relevant details on his communication system, to his waiting colleagues on the spacecraft, still positioned above the earth.

A year later, the alien returned to earth and thanked Jane Clarke for her valuable help. He confirmed that his species had found most cures for their ailments and that they had started to breed once more.

Jane thanked him and asked a question. 'What were the illnesses your species had,' she asked.

'In your language, the alien replied, we have now cured Malaria, Influenza, Cholera and smallpox. We think all these and other illnesses were given to our species over the years, following our visits to all the countries on earth, when we were planning to attack and dominate the world.'

'And now, Jane asked, are you still planning to invade our planet and take us over?'

'Not at the moment he replied, but we are watching some of the countries who are building up their Atomic Weapons, and should any of these despotic leaders decide to wage a nuclear war, we will have to return and ensure that the earth will survive and be a peaceful place to live!'

Jane sighed with relief and gave her thanks to her alien friend and his donation, for the product that was now being used worldwide, a product that would be produced,

and used as a cure for a majority of illnesses, with the brand name, which would be known as "*LIFEBLOOD*"!

16: MISSING!

It was late afternoon, on Tuesday May 30th, 1972, the day after the Spring Bank Holiday, when five friends had been looking forward to getting together, at the Battersea Park, Pleasure Gardens, to enjoy the rides, which were either of

British manufacture, or from America.

The boys, who were still in most of their school uniforms, but without ties and caps, wandered from the main gate, on the Queenstown Road roundabout, and then into the park.

As they followed most of the people along the pathways, they decided to take out a dinghy, onto the large boating lake, before continuing to the pleasure gardens. They paid the man in the kiosk, to take two dinghies onto the large lake, where, after just two-minutes, were shouted at, by one of the attendants, telling them to "sit down", or they would be asked to leave the park; so they only used the small crafts for 15-minutes, as they all agreed that rowing was hard work!

They followed the pathway, alongside the river Thames, and spotted the small, narrow-gauge railway, and then, the tree-walk, which they used, to take them across to the pleasure gardens funfair entrance, from the river side.

They walked quickly past the water gardens, and the Guinness Clock, as it was the rides in the funfair, that they wanted to use, after hearing so much about them from their schoolmates.

As soon as they entered the funfair, they spotted the Big Dipper, which was a wooden roller-coaster, with very steep inclines, and very noisy carriages, when they were on their descent, at a very high speed!

They agreed that they would try the "Rotor" first, which was a scary experience for all of them, but nobody would own up to being scared, as that wasn't the way to show your friends that you were being scared, but all of them breathed a sigh of relief, when the ride had stopped spinning, as the smell of the rubber made everyone feel quite sick!

The boys then separated, as some of them wanted to use the "Big-Dipper" roller coaster, and the others said they would save it for later.

Robin Mason was aged 13, and lived in Clapham Junction, with his parents, a brother and a sister, who were both older than him. Robin and his older brother, went to Spencer Park Secondary Modern School, in Trinity Road, Wandsworth, where Robin had decided to join the technical studies, rather than the academic studies, as he eventually wanted to follow his father into the car business, where he enjoyed "tinkering" with all types of cars. His mother Carol, worked at the South London Hospital, in Clapham South, as a part-time Auxiliary nurse, which she enjoyed, as it would keep her busy for 3-weekdays, but no weekends, and travelling was easy from Clapham Junction, in her small, blue Austin 1100 car.

Robin had spoken to some of his friends at school, and had arranged with four of them, to meet at the gates of Battersea Park, and that they would go after school had finished, on Tuesday, 30th May.

Robin Mason, and his best mate Brian Ford, went on the dodgem cars, the big-wheel, the helter-skelter, and the carousel, but both of them were anxious to climb aboard the infamous, wooden big-dipper!

Brian spotted their three other friends, who were in the queue, when one of the boys shouted at them, saying that they had saved a place for them, but chose to ignore the "huffing and puffing", coming from the people, who were queuing behind them.

The five friends took up the three rear carriages of the ride, where Robin and Brian had taken the very last carriage, and their other friends, who had managed to sit in the two compartments in front of them.

Robin looked at the structure of the wooden ride, from over his carriage, and noticed that some of the timber looked as though it was rotting away, but knowing that the ride had been in use for a long time, didn't think any more about it.

The train was released, and started to climb very slowly, up to the highest point of the track, by a haulage rope, then once it had reached the peak, the brakeman applied the "rollback" brake, but it didn't engage. He tried several times to get the brake to work, but without success! The entire train swiftly descended backwards, causing the rear carriage to jump away from the rails, then to crash through the barrier, together with the two connected carriages, crashing on top of it!

All five friends were in these carriages, and they were either thrown over the side, or had managed to cling onto the side of the track.

Below the big-dipper roller-coaster ride, there were shouts and screams, that could be heard all across the entire park. There were some lifeless bodies lying on the ground, below the ride, and also, a number of people who had injuries, that required urgent attention.

Several ambulances and police cars arrived; the medics treated the injured, before taking them into the awaiting ambulances. The police officers had placed blankets over the persons who were pronounced as dead; which amounted to a total of five young people.

Three of the friends, who had been in the carriages in front of Robin and Brian's rear compartment, had managed to escape with just the odd bruise, and were being checked over by one of the nurses, who had just arrived, when they looked at the five covered bodies, and wondered whether their other two friends were amongst them.

The policemen were checking the covered bodies for any identification, so that their parents could be notified as soon as possible, then one of the five friends, Robert, walked over and asked if they had found their two missing friends, who were named Robin Mason and Brian Ford?

Robert was told that they had identified everyone, and that neither Robin, or Brian were amongst the dead, but he would ask one of his colleagues to check on the injured persons. The officer returned and told Robert, that Brian Ford had been taken to hospital, but there was nobody called Robin Mason, amongst the injured!

 The police officer announced to a waiting reporter, that five children had died at the scene of the roller coaster ride, and that a further thirteen people had been injured, and taken to hospital, which was overheard by Robert Ottaway, aged 13, one of the five school friends, who had come to Battersea Park, that day, on 30th May.

The parents of the boys had been contacted by the police, and arrived at the funfair, to pick up their sons. Mrs. Ford was asked to attend the St James Hospital in Balham, but had contacted her friend Carol, Robins mother, to discuss the tragic incident. Carol Mason was shocked, she hadn't been contacted by the police, as her son was not amongst the dead or injured, so she drove to Battersea Park, to see if she could find him.

A frantic Carol Mason searched, then showed a photo of her son to the medics, and the police officers, and asked them if they had seen her son Robin, but a police officer informed her, that he was not listed as being one of the unfortunate victims, and must be somewhere close by?

Carol spotted Robins three friends, who were now with their parents, and asked them about what happened, and whether they knew where Robin was, but they each explained that the roller coaster went backwards, and threw people out of their carriages, and would have been unable to see exactly what actually occurred, as they were facing forward. Carol was upset, and was comforted by one of the medics. 'My son was on the rear carriage of that roller coaster, said Carol, and he is not here, so where is he?'

Carol continued to search the park, but it was now getting darker, so she went back to the scene, and gave her telephone number to one of the police officers, hoping that they would contact her, if Robin was found.

The daily papers were full of photos and stories about the tragic incident, the following day, and some of the newspapers had managed to get some further details over the events. In one of the papers, an eye-witness had reported that one of the boys, who had been seated in the rear carriage, had gone missing, but his friend, who had sat next to him, was taken to hospital, due to his injuries.

Carol and her husband Bill, were distraught, they hadn't heard from anyone over the disappearance of their son, so

Carol rang her friend Jennie, Brian Fords mother, to see whether Brian could offer any more details about the time of the accident.

'The carriage went backwards at high speed, said Brian, then the last thing I remember, was that both myself and Robin were thrown out of the car, then I saw Robin, who was clinging onto one of the timber barriers, but I cannot remember anything more, as I had somehow landed at the base of the big-dipper, then I blacked out?'

Carol thanked Brian, and said she wished him well, but asked him to call her, if he remembered anything else. Jennie, Brian's mother, told Carol to check with the police, to see if they had any more details, as the inquest was due to be carried out, in a few days.

Carol, and her husband Bill, arrived at the Nine-Elms Police Station, and spoke to the Detective Inspector, who was dealing with the case, who told them that their enquires were still ongoing, and that no further evidence about their son had been found, and that they still awaited statements from other persons, who had been at the funfair, on 30th May. 'What do we do now said Carol, we can't move forward, until we know what has happened?'

Detective Inspector Broughton, offered his condolences, and said that he would be attending a service for their missing son, at Spencer Park School, which was planned for Monday 5th June, and that he would try and gather more information before then.

The service was held in the chapel, by the old building, at Spencer Park Secondary Modern School, in Wandsworth, and was carried out by the Headmaster, Mr. Turner, who read a short passage from the bible, then asked everyone to stand, so that they could sing "Holy, Holy, Holy, Lord God Almighty", which Robin's music teacher had confirmed as one of the boy's favourite hymns. Tears were shed from the most of the teachers and parents, including Robin's mother Carol, and her friend Jennifer Ford, whose sons had been at the funfair that day.

DI Broughton spoke to Carol Mason, after the service and apologised, when he told her that his Chief Inspector had asked him to close the case, due to no further evidence, and that the case would be classed as a "Missing Person"!

Carol told the officer that she wouldn't sleep, until her son had been found, but realised that without any evidence, the police were unable to continue. Carol spoke to her husband Bill, later that day, who was unable to attend the service, due to ill health, and she told him about the police officer's comments, but Bill said he knew this was coming, but together, they would continue their search for Robin.

At the Battersea Park Pleasure Gardens, the remains of the big-dipper had been dismantled, and taken to a council storage depot, somewhere close by.

The actual site, where the redundant materials were, was never revealed, and the London Borough of Wandsworth, allegedly had these remains, buried below the site of the ride.

A month later, six-weeks after the Pleasure Gardens incident, Bill Mason, Robin's father, was rushed into St James hospital, in Balham, following a suspected heart-attack, and was taken to the Intensive Care unit, where he was monitored closely. Carol had been working that morning, at the South-London hospital, and was alerted by the ward sister, so she left straight away, and drove the short journey, within five-minutes.

The nurse on duty, informed Carol that her husband was comfortable, but would need some surgery, to alleviate the pressure on his heart, which made Carol quite upset, knowing that her son Robin was missing, and now, it was possible that her husband may be in danger of losing his life. Carol stayed in the hospital and helped where she could, just to take her mind away from the current problems, and saw her husband being taken back to the Intensive Care unit. She gripped his hand and held it, until he was returned to his place in the ward, then started to speak to him, even though he was still under the anesthetic.

Bill Mason was out for the count, he was fast asleep, but inside his mind, he could see himself floating down a dark alleyway, where he saw several pairs of hands, trying to grab him. He continued to float aimlessly along, but he could hear something, which sounded like a voice, which he found calming at first, but as it got louder, it became menacing; then four pairs of hands grabbed him tightly, trying to stop him from moving! Bill was still floating, but was static, something had stopped him, but he couldn't feel the hands, that had grabbed him earlier. The voice had stopped, so he was just left, in what he assumed was somewhere between "life and death", but without knowing whether he was alive or dead, he had to wait for the outcome.

The place he was in became brighter, and as he started to move again, he saw what he thought was a fairground, with music playing, and the sight of a helter-skelter, a carousel, and a crowd of people, who were looking above, at one of the other rides, the Big-Dipper Roller Coaster!

Carol could see that her husband was having difficulties, and called the nurse, who took his blood-pressure, and then sent a bleeped message, for a doctor to attend. The doctor checked Bill over, but was happy with his progress, and assured Carol that it was a natural occurrence, after surgery, that the body would move about, but that they would keep checking him, at regular intervals.

Bill was still inside the fairground, he could see that people had fallen from the big dipper, and that some of these were injured, or worse, but he couldn't move, or speak!

Carol watched again, as her husband started moving from side to side, and called the nurse again. The nurse had been told by the doctor, to give the patient a calming drug, by injection, if he went into spasm again, so she injected the drug through the canula, which soon made Bill calm down.

Bill was still watching the activity, above and below the big dipper, when he thought he could see his son Robin; he could see a strange dark figure, who was dressed in a dark suit, with a long dark coat, draped across his shoulders. The dark figure was carrying his son, but he couldn't see where he was taking him, then the lighting faded, the funfair started to vanish, then he woke up!

'Carol, I have seen Robin, shouted Bill, he is still in the funfair, he is safe!' Carol grabbed his hand and called the nurse, but asked her husband what he was talking about, as all she could hear was the words, "funfair", and "safe", but these were distorted words, when he was shouting them out?

The nurse checked Bill over, just before the doctor arrived, and Carol asked about what he was saying. The doctor arrived, and said that her husband was still under the effects of the anesthetic, and had probably been dreaming about something, as he was starting to become conscious, so Carol thought no more about it, as Bill had gone back to sleep.

Bill Mason was released from hospital two-weeks later, and was asked to take things easy for at least a month, so Carol took some time off from her job, so that she could take care of her husband, until he showed signs of being independent. One afternoon, Carol had made a pot of tea, as she knew her friend Jennie was coming round to see how Bill was. Carol told her husband that he had a visitor, as Jennie popped her head round the lounge door, then gave him a quick kiss and asked how he was. 'I saw what happened, said Bill, I was there, at the funfair, and saw the dead children, I also saw our son Robin!'

Jennie looked at Carol, and asked if Bill was taking any medication, as it would probably make him dream, but Bill spoke again. 'I saw Robin, he is safe!'

Carol started to get upset, and wondered why her husband had said he'd seen their son, then remembered when he was in the Intensive Care Unit, when he called out the words, "safe and funfair", then wondered whether he had actually seen something.

Bill kept quiet until Jennie had left, then explained to his wife about what he had witnessed, when he was in hospital. Carol checked that he hadn't taken more medication than he should have, but saw that he'd taken nothing since breakfast. 'I will go to the park tomorrow, said Carol; if there is a chance he is still there, then I will find him!'

Bill felt uneasy, and didn't want to tell her about the dark figure, but he was still not 100% fit, so he wasn't able to do anything.

Derek Ford, Jennies husband and Brian's father, called round a bit later, to see Bill and Carol, after her friend Jennie, had told her husband about what he had said. 'I will go to the park with Carol, and together, we can search the area's you have described; let's hope we can find Robin!'

Bill asked Carol to get Derek a drink, then when she had left the room, Bill told Derek that there were dark forces involved here, and didn't want them to get hurt, so it may be too dangerous, if just the two of them went to the park, so it was agreed, that Derek would contact the other three fathers, and a few friends, so that they could check the areas, this coming weekend. 'I will come with you all, said Bill, he is my son, and I want him back, whatever the cost!'

On the Saturday morning, five men arrived at the funfair, where they would commence the search, based on what Bill had explained. They were met by Detective Inspector Broughton, who had been contacted by Bill, as he wanted him to bring some back-up officers, in case of any violence.

DI Broughton wasn't convinced, all he could make out, was that Bill Mason had seen something, when he was under the effects of the anesthetic, and other drugs, and that the dark forces were behind the disappearance of Robin Mason, so it would have been very hard to convince his Chief Inspector, with that sort of information, so he couldn't bring any back up officers with him, that morning.

DI Broughton had arranged with the funfair manager, to gain access into the grounds, before the public arrived, but had been told that they had only two-hours, then the gates would be opened.

Four of the fathers split up, and searched the vicinity of the grounds, where the big dipper used to be; Bill and DI Broughton went together, to the area seen in the dream, which would have been the exact spot, that Robin had allegedly been seen, by his father, when he was undergoing surgery.

They had all been searching for nearly an hour, then DI Broughton looked up at the water-chute ride, thinking that he'd seen something, so the funfair manager gave the officer access into the attraction, and followed him up to the top of the ride. DI Broughton looked over at the site where the big dipper had been, and once again, saw something, but this time, he could clearly see a see a strange dark figure, who was dressed in a dark suit, with a long dark coat, draped across his shoulders. The two men returned to the base of the water-chute, as fast as they could, but there was nobody there. 'I clearly saw something,' stated DI Broughton, then continued to search the area. Bill Mason checked with the other fathers, but nobody had seen anything.

One of the fathers lit up a cigarette, and sat on one of the benches, at the rear of the rotor, which was just in front of the old big dipper site. Bill Mason noticed that there was a manhole behind the bench, which looked as though it had not been secured, so he called DI Broughton, and the funfair manager over, to ask if somebody could lift the cover, as he remembered seeing this, in his dream.

The cover was lifted, then they saw some dark clothing, which was screwed up tight, looking as though it was there to stop the flow of water. The funfair manager used a 2-way radio, to contact the maintenance manager, then 5-minutes later, two stocky men, dressed in dungarees appeared, and were asked to check the drainage system. 'Where does the water go to from here,' asked DI Broughton?

The two maintenance men led them to a medium sized pumping station, which was positioned close to the river Thames. The maintenance man found the keys, but confirmed that the door was unlocked. Inside the room, they saw some scraps of food, and some bones, but these were not human, then one of the men lifted an inspection cover, just outside the pumping station, and saw something hideous, and crouching at the entrance to one of the gullies. *'You, out,'* shouted DI Broughton!

The creature was very dark, and looked like a large dog, but it had deformed hands and feet, and a large body, once it had shown its full self.

The creature was covered in a slimy mixture of grease and oil, and wore only a small towel, which was wrapped around its lower body; its teeth were stained, and small scraps of food were trapped between some of the gaps.

The creature leapt upwards, and landed on its two feet, which startled the two maintenance men, then DI Broughton removed his jacket, and placed it over the cowering body. 'Where is the boy, asked Bill Mason, where is my son?'

The creature ignored Bill at first, but then pointed at the gulley. 'Is he down there, asked Bill, is he alive?'

DI Broughton radioed his boss, and advised him over what they had found, and asked for transport, to take the creature somewhere, where it could be questioned.

The officer asked the maintenance men if they could provide a plan of the gullies, so one of them went back to his office in the park grounds, and returned shortly after, with a bundle of rolled up plans.

Four builders arrived, together with a small digger, then, after checking the layouts of the buried gullies, started to dig down, approximately 30-feet away, from the pumping station.

The digger removed enough earth from the area, and revealed the side of a pump-room, and continued digging around the room, so that someone could access it.

One of the builders produced a band-saw, then proceeded to cut an aperture into the side of the steel room; he made a small square hole, so that he could see inside, then was passed a large torch. As he peered through the aperture, he could see a pair of eyes, and a very greasy face, which stared at him! *'Dad?'*

Bill Mason could hear his son calling out to him, from the pump room below, but was asked to stand clear, so that the builder could enlarge the aperture, and release the boy.

Robin Mason was finally released from the pump room, but he was not alone; there were three other boys with him, all of whom were in the same greasy condition, but blankets were handed out, by the police and medics, who had been called to the scene, by DI Broughton.

Bill cuddled his son briefly, but was told by one of the doctors, that he should be given a quick check. All four boys were checked over, and pronounced as being healthy, but very hungry.

Carol Mason arrived, after being picked up by a police woman; she ran over to Robin, who was sitting in the back of one of the ambulances, and wept tears of joy, once she saw her lost son.

The creature, who had been hiding below ground, was a

man, who was approximately forty-years of age, and had a mental disorder, which meant that his body had become deformed, and had also taken away his ability to speak; the man was then placed into a "Black-Maria", and taken away from the park.

An inquest was held, a few days later, where it was established that Robin Mason had been thrown from the rear carriage of the big dipper roller coaster, and had managed to land on a pile of rubbish, close to the bench, then was abducted and drugged, by a mentally disturbed man, and imprisoned below the grassy area, within a pump room, that was barely big enough to house the four boys, and their captor.

The three other boys, who were aged fourteen, to sixteen-years of age, and found at the scene, were homeless, and without any parents, and were living inside the grounds of Battersea Park, where they too, were drugged, and abducted by the deformed man, so there was nobody to contact, to advise that they were safe.

The deformed man, who was named as Mr. Smith, was sent to a mental institute, somewhere in Epsom, Surrey, and due to his illness, was not charged with the abduction of four boys.

Robin took weeks to regain his strength and mental stability, but returned to Spencer Park School after the summer holidays, to continue with his studies.

After the accident, on May 30th 1972, the Big Dipper Roller Coaster was closed and dismantled, and with the funfair's lack of a main attraction its use soon declined, leading to its closure in 1974. Very little remains now to even suggest that a funfair once stood on the site!

Printed in Great Britain
by Amazon

86601450R00122